MW00874543

70

METERS

RYAN SNIDER

READYAIMWRITE
kids

READYAIMWRITE
kids

70 Meters

Ryan Snider
Copyedited and typeset by Rebecca Millen

www.KidsWriteStories.net

First U.S. Edition, 2021-12-15

ISBN: 979-8-9850348-2-0
Printed in the U.S.A.

*This book is dedicated to
my brother, my family, friends,
and everyone else who
supported me all the way.*

Thank you.

Atlantis will rise again.

~ Charles Olson

70
METERS

TABLE OF CONTENTS

CHAPTER ONE
A FLOATING STONE

We all knew it was coming. They told us about what would happen, how the world would change. But we didn't listen. Some did, they moved inland and tried to stop it, tried to fight the multibillion-dollar corporations around the globe who were slowly, painfully, cooking the Earth.

It was small for the first dozen years or so, a tenth of a degree higher here, a ton or so from ice to water, high tide a foot higher. No one paid much attention. Then, it got bad. A hundred years later, Category Six hurricanes slammed into every major continent on Earth, killing millions and flooding coastal areas on a scale of biblical proportions. 'It's just a freak incident,' they said. But no, people were scared now. Like Dr. Frankenstein, they saw the horror of their creation too late. Humankind was doomed.

It started with the Arctic, raising the sea a couple of feet. Then Greenland, Northern Canada, Alaska, Russia. The sea churned as the ice crashed into it. Florida, Louisiana, Georgia, Alabama, Texas, North Carolina, South Carolina, Hawaii, Cuba, The Caribbean, The

Bahamas – all disappeared within days, sometimes mere hours. Then Antarctica. One of the largest continents in the world, holding 5.4 million square miles of ice, dumped it all into the ocean. Parts of California, New England, Canada, Brazil, Chile, Argentina, the UK, India, Australia, The Philippines, Japan, Africa, Russia, Europe – covered in endless expanses of water.

But that was sixty years ago. Now, only the rich and powerful own land. After their huge companies were swallowed by waves, they moved to the highest ground possible and kicked everyone out, forcing them to the barren coasts and the ocean beyond.

My name is Dylan Stone. I am the sixteen-year-old son of Chief Poseidon Stone, the leader of our raft city we call New Atlantis. I've lived on this raft my whole life, only seeing the land once, when we were casting off, and I was very young. I've always wanted to go on the land, but my father said it's too dangerous. The land-dwellers would kill me or make me a slave, endlessly toiling away wherever they choose. But I have to go. I'm bored of seeing the same waves rock our raft over and over and *over*. The Elders tell stories of before the Floods, where the ocean kissed the land at places called beaches, where soft, white sand stretched for miles, turning into lush green gardens and towering, glamorous *hotels*. They tell stories of gentle hills becoming giant mountains, mating the land with the sky. The deep canyons in comparison, made by water flowing through the rock. Deserts, near-endless expanses of sand without water. Snow, *frozen water*, falling from the sky and giving them joy, the fun times with friends and family. It doesn't snow on the ocean. The only mountains are shifting titans of water, the only *sand* deep beneath the surface. I'm currently dangling off the edge of our highest building, our flagpole in the center of New Atlantis, erected on top of our Council building. Only a couple dozen feet above the water, I can see so much up here, my dirty blonde hair whipping around in the salty wind. So much water, that is.

CHAPTER TWO
SHADOW OF THE FUTURE

"Dylan!"

I looked down, and saw Alex, my best friend, waving up at me, her hand blocking the sun, brown hair blowing slightly in the wind.

"What's up?" I yelled back, holding onto the pole with one hand, swinging down to the roof. I jumped down onto the raft floor with a hollow wooden *thunk*. "What's up?" I repeated.

She smiled, her telltale smirk making me smile. "What are you doing up there?"

I shrugged. We began walking. "Oh, y'know. Just looking."

"For what?" she asked, stepping in front of me. "Water?"

I laughed and pushed her aside. "Land, genius. You wouldn't know, because you're getting to see it in, like, two days."

It was true. Alex was a JT, or Junior Trader. Eventually, she would be responsible for keeping trade partners with the other rafts and stabilizing the fragile system with the land-dwellers. She would get to see *land*. Meanwhile, I'm stuck here learning how to become the next Chief.

"Oh, relax," she said, lightly punching my shoulder. "I'll tell you all about it."

"But I don't want to be *told*," I whined. She really knew how to hit nerves. "I want to *see*."

We had made our way to the southern edge of New Atlantis, and I leaned against the wooden railing, the familiar wooden *creak* soothing. Off in the distance, a huge wall of storm clouds was gathering, lightning crackling inside it.

"Alex!" Her brother, Abel, came running up. He took a sidelong glance at me before continuing. "Chief Poseidon has ordered the Traders to leave a day early. He doesn't want anyone trapped in that storm."

Alex turned back to me and grabbed my hand. "Wish me luck," she said, and took off, the wind picking up. I never got to reply.

CHAPTER THREE
THE REBEL SON

Half an hour before the ships left, my father called a citywide meeting at the Capitol Building.

"Ladies and gentlemen, a storm is coming. I have sent the Traders on their way, and they should be leaving shortly. However, we must be careful. We are following the Eastern Ridge, coming around south to the Gulf Passage. You know that storms in these areas are hard, and we are dangerously close to land. As such, this

9

meeting is a warning. Secure all knots and lashings. Tie everything down. We're in for a ride."

And that was that. The trading ships cast off, their huge sails unfurling in the wind, the great wooden hulls creaking, old engines roaring. Not a minute after the last ship leaves, we begin our breakup into the nine Districts of New Atlantis. If I've never told you what Atlantis looks like, forgive me. It's shaped like a large oval, with slightly more rectangular edges than a circle. Mostly, it's made out of wood, some plastic, sheet metal, pretty much anything they found that would float. The outer Districts are newer, made of more wood, better structure. When we break for a storm, we split

New Atlantis in half down the long side, then cut the halves into three separate sections, and voila, nine ships, nine Districts. Now, it's not all even, as my dad wanted these pieces to be as aerodynamic as possible, to conserve fuel. I barely know how this stuff works. It's just cool as the city splits apart, water rushing in and between the pieces.

The sea begins to churn as the sky darkens. As the rain starts, I climb down from the roof of my house into the Spearhead District. My conversation with Alex resurfaces in my mind, simultaneously reigniting an old question. I find my father in his Chief's robe.

"Dad," I said. "When are we going back to land?"

The wind began to howl, and the raft began to creak. He turns to me.

"Son, we've talked about this. The land is not safe."

"So, why send the Traders there?"

Dad sighed and laid his robe on his bed, rain hammering the roof.

"We don't have everything here, so we need to trade with the land-dwellers. It's dangerous, but necessary. How many more times-"

"I want to go on land."

My dad's eyes drill into me, his demeanor as Chief Poseidon darkening the room.

"Dylan," he said. "I've told you no. The land is dangerous. They killed your mother! Our home is the sea."

12

"It's not my home, Dad!" I yelled, lightning striking the ocean on cue. He took a step back, startled by my outburst. "I want to go on land! All the stories the Elders told us; the land was beautiful!"

"The land is death!" Dad roared. Lightning crackled through the window behind him, and I saw nothing but water rearing up to strike.

"DAD!" I dove forward, arms outstretched. The water burst through the window and flared, like hitting an invisible wall, before another wave collapsed on top of us.

CHAPTER FOUR
A NEW LEGACY

"Dylan? Dylan! Dylan!" Rough hands jolted me awake, and harsh sunlight stabbed my eyes. A dark figure grabs my arm and pulls me up. My eyes adjust, and I see the wreckage around us. New Atlantis is still in one piece, the districts haphazardly put back together.

"What, what happened?" I asked the figure, who turned out to be Azul, my father's advisor. The ocean blue eyes that gave him his name turned on me.

"The storm," he said, not a man of many words. His wife, Kalama, came up beside me.

"It almost broke New Atlantis apart," she said in her soothing voice. "The wave that hit destroyed the Capitol, almost wiped Spearhead out."

The nagging feeling in my stomach rose up like bile. The words caught in my throat.

"Where's my father?" I asked. "Dad?"

Azul placed a calloused hand on my shoulder.

"We can't find him. He must have been taken by the sea."

I collapse to my knees. My father, the indestructible Chief Poseidon, is gone. His last words fill my head, his disembodied voice booming. *The land is death!* I add, with a sickening truth, a second sentence. *But the sea is merciless.*

I turn back to the wreckage, a glint catching my eye. There, buried in the rubble, is my father's ceremonial trident. He never used it much; it only saw the sun during important events and ceremonies. Like the death of a chief, or the crowning of another. Kalama sees me and picks it up.

"It's yours now, Dylan," she said. "You are the new chief. The new Poseidon."

I take the trident, its sharp points seeming to pierce the air. The others have noticed, and are gathering around. Azul's voice booms over the crowd.

"The Chief is dead!" he said, the abrupt verdict like a fishing hook in my throat. "Dylan Stone has become the new Chief Poseidon!"

"*Wait!*"

A voice breaks over the crowd. Ezra comes forward. He was once my father's friend, turned harshest critic. Now his dark eyes turn on me.

"How do we know this *boy* is ready to lead?"

Murmurs rise from the crowd like bubbles coming to the surface. Azul opens his mouth to speak, but I jump ahead of him.

"How dare you," I said, my voice hard as rock. I come up close to him, gripping the trident tightly. "My father is dead. It is my duty to take his place."

Ezra smiles and takes a step back.

"Dear boy, that's where you're wrong. Your father was the first chief we've ever had. And I am not going to allow New Atlantis to become one of the land's monarchies of old." He turns to the crowd and raises his fist. "We are a new nation!" His response is shouts of agreement. He turns back to me. "But, Dylan, if you are chief, then where are the ships?"

A second pang of fear buries into my chest.

"They should be safe," I said. "They only left yesterday."

A loud gasp erupts from the crowd, and I know I've made a mistake. Ezra smiles. I fell into his trap.

"Oh no, my dear Chief," he said. "They left *two days* ago. The storm was longer than it was to you, huh?"

My head whips around to Azul, whose ocean-blue eyes have lost some of their color. He slowly shakes his head. *Why didn't you tell me, Azul?*

"You know the code, Chief," Ezra said. "Send a message, via bird, for status, *daily*. And I can't help but wonder, my Chief, where is the update?"

I whirl around, praying to see one of the Scouts holding up a piece of paper, but nothing. Ezra shakes his head at my panic. The crowd has begun to murmur again, the fear consuming me. Finally, Ezra strikes.

"Go, Dylan!" he yelled, startling everyone. "Find the ships. Since you cannot be trusted with the duties of a chief, I shall take over." He grabs my trident and shoves me away roughly. "By the power vested in me as Head of the Council and Chief Poseidon, I hereby declare *Dylan Stone* to be exiled until he proves himself worthy and returns with the Traders, *and their ships*." He smiled, the dark smile of a man who accomplished his mission.

Kalama and Azul help me up, but my head is pounding. No, this can't be happening. *No, no, no, no!*

Azul whispers in my ear, "I go with you."

We turn around and walk toward the aft of the city when Ezra speaks.

"My dear boy, you must go *alone*, you know…"

Finally, Azul speaks.

"He is a boy! I must go with him, as his father's advisor."

"You mean *my* advisor?" Ezra laughs, as the fight is drawn out of Azul. He is nothing if not loyal to the city.

I break away from Kalama and run toward the docks, Ezra's haunting laugh behind me.

CHAPTER FIVE
THE LOST PRINCE

Azul and Kalama did what they could, but it was futile. Ezra exiled me, on a doomed mission, to find my doomed people. Right now, the only things left to the Stone name were a battered fishing boat and a rusted fishing trident.

It's been a day. Ezra was *kind* enough to loan me a map so I could 'find my way.' The Traders had been heading to the Eastern Ridge, part of the continent of America. We were almost at the Gulf Passage when the storm hit, so if I'm lucky, I should hit the coast before day three. Day four the gas would run out.

Hit the coast. I don't know why, but my thoughts keep drifting to seeing land, not the Traders, not Alex. It feels like my mind has been shattered ever since the storm, like the damage it did was more than physical. I set the boat's course and headed to the aft of my 15-foot vessel of destiny. The dark blue water churned under the noon sun, agitated by my boat's motor. The wind blew hard, whipped by the rough, rusted lines of the ship. It was just us out here, just me and my boat.

Thin, wind-battered clouds slice the sky. I look up, and notice a small streak slowly grazing across the sky. A small, almost imperceptible black dot leads the trail. Then, the dot cut a large curve across the sky, then turned into an angle.

Wait. It's coming down. The realization hit me as stories from the Elders came up. They used to have machines called airplanes, which could carry a man, and a bunch of people, into the sky. This must be an airplane. I ran to the bridge and cut off the engine, going adrift.

A loud whooshing drone filled the air as the airplane leveled out. I could see it more clearly now, and it's not like anything the Elders told me. This one didn't have the large wings, the long body... *fuselage*, I think. It was smaller, with wings angled against the body, and a sharp, deadly-looking nose. I stood on the bow, waving my hands. Suddenly, it tilted upward and slowed, spraying water everywhere and rocking my boat. Now it was only thirty feet from my ship. It hovered there, a whooshing sound filling my head. Then, part of the nose slid back, revealing a person sitting in a chair. A crackly voice boomed out from the airplane.

"Who are you and what is your business trespassing on Cainscion waters?" Startled, I take a step back.

"My name is Dylan Stone!" I shout over the engine. "I am from the city of New Atlantis, and I'm looking for our trading ships! We lost them in a storm; they should have been to the land by now!"

"Follow me. I will have escorts at your position soon." The airplane crackled, and rose up above my boat.

"Wait!" I said. "How am I supposed to follow you?"

The airplane's engines roared as it shot into the sky, leaving a long white trail for me to follow.

CHAPTER SIX
ESCORTS TO DEATH

It took an hour for Death to find me. But when he did, he came in the form of huge metal ships, monsters with huge guns. I saw Death, and he looked at me, and he pitied me, so Death let me pass.

Why am I in a poetic mood? No idea. All the Elders on New Atlantis spoke in ancient riddles. My mind has been lying in pieces, holding on to the last shards of good life on Atlantis. I can't handle Ezra's betrayal. It feels so wrong, when I look back at it. Like it was planned, forced, but it happened nonetheless. The great metal behemoths towered over my puny boat, and it took another hour to reach shore.

There was no fanfare or fireworks, no sloping beaches and glamourous hotels. Rather, before we reached land, we had to travel through Death's domain.

Huge towers, some as tall as the New Atlantis Capitol, jutted out of the ocean, leaning at odd angles. We had to weave our way through, the towers becoming silent guardians, covered in moss. The towers slowly fell back into the ocean as we left what once might have been a bustling metropolis.

Then, more buildings rose from the waters, shorter and wider, funneling us through the black waters. I saw huge, gnarled twists of wood, and a word flashed through my mind. *Trees*. The Elders told stories of how the world was once full of them, how they were tall and grand, majestic and powerful.

The trees I saw did not look majestic. Their... *branches*... stretched into the sky, like a dying hand reaching into the clouds, a cry out for help that was never heard. Chills ran down my spine as my boat was thrown in the shadows of my escorts, their huge guns unwavering.

Then I saw it. A huge wall, twice as tall as the metal ships were long, made from the same featureless metal, save for the huge rivets and seams not unlike those on the Trader ships' engines. It stretched for miles; I couldn't see the end of it. Near the water, the wall remained untouched, strangely lacking swaths of algae and barnacles. A gate built for Titans towers above me, and it swings open as we approach, the metal releasing a bone-chilling moan as we sail through. The gunships went through first, their wake making my boat rock, sending waves crashing against the inside of the Wall.

We came out on the other side into a huge, sprawling city.

CHAPTER SEVEN
GOLD BANDS

I was pulled into a huge harbor, my senses assaulted by light and sound. Dozens of ships were pulled up to the docks, like us. Buildings towered off in the distance, disappearing into the clouds. People milled around the docks, carrying tools, weapons, cases. It was mesmerizing. My escorts led me to the far right of the docks, where similar ships were stationed. I felt puny, compared to these megalithic monsters, but I gripped my trident tightly, and slung my bag over my shoulder. I would not show fear, for my name was Stone.

I slowly guided my boat to a dock next to my escorts when my ship lurched. I was thrown to the deck, and my ship began to rise into the sky. I scrambled to the edge, where I saw that my boat was attached to a metallic pad, about a foot thick and almost as wide as my hull. The pad was rigged to a small tower of thick scaffolding and a stone-looking material, and I saw similar structures lining the docks. My boat rose over the water, stopping when my deck was level with… a second dock?

There was a second floor built above the sea-level docks, supported by the metal-and-stone beams where the pads were connected. It seemed to be a… a… gathering area… for people on the ships. Metal groaned underneath me, and my jaw dropped as the gunships beside me began to rise, with at least half a dozen pads lifting them the twenty-or-so feet to this second floor. I stared in awe as the pads stopped with a *thunk*, and people, no, soldiers, began filing off the ship. I had never seen so many people in one place before.

Five of the soldiers, guns out, boarded my ship. My knuckles were white from gripping my trident. One of them had a bright yellow band on his forearm, almost gold. Probably their leader.

"Aerial reports show your vessel violated

Cainscion waters and our sovereign borders. And according to the Cainscion Justice Marks, any unidentified vessel found in Cainscion territory shall be immediately referred to as hostile, captured, and subject to trial. Sorry sir, but you need to come with us."

The leader stepped aside, and a gangplank extended from the building to my deck. The rest automatically tightened their grips on their rifles, as if they've done this before, with less… civilized interactions. I stay still and silent for a while, my trident in one hand, my bag in the other. The leader sighs quietly and gives an almost imperceptible nod. Two of the soldiers behind him move forward, and I take a step back.

"I am registered," I said, surprising them. "I come from New Atlantis, in search of our trade ships. They've passed through here recently, but got lost in a storm."

One of them glances back at the gold-banded man, who nods. They yank the trident from my hand, and the other shoves my hands behind my back. A third hit me in the face with his gun, making stars dance across my vision. The gold-banded man knelt and whispered.

"Cainscion doesn't recognize New Atlantis and the other raft cities as sovereign nations, *fish*. Especially here in Enoch Harbor. Your kind are pathetic, losers who abandoned the land."

That was the last I heard before I blacked out.

CHAPTER EIGHT
THE CONSTABLE

The walls around me brightened from an abyssal black to the dull grey of stone. I didn't know where I was, but this must be the 'captured and subject to trial' the gold-banded man said. Strange. The trials on New Atlantis were different. The accused wouldn't be thrown in the brig until they were convicted. An alarm buzzed, and a thick door on the opposite wall opened, a little indicator light turning green. A pair of guards walked in, their armbands a deep red. Their faces were hidden behind a stark black mask, with a thin white stripe running across the helmet where their eyes would be. Without a word, they grabbed me and lifted me up, my head still spinning. They dragged me through a dim hallway, my feet pulling uselessly along behind me. I was still trying to remember where I was. My eyes closed once again.

I found myself in a large, ornate courtroom. I knew what they looked like because we had one in New Atlantis. It was nothing like this, just a simple chair for the chief and small stands for the citizens, with a side for the… *prosecutor and defendant*. This place was very different from New Atlantis. There was a large chair in the front of the room, almost like a throne, situated behind a tall wooden desk. It seemed like everything here… in *Cainscion*, was larger-than life. My captors hooked my cuffs to a thick ringbolt hammered into the floor, so I could do nothing but kneel. The thought churned in my head, the anger giving me focus. I took a deep breath and looked around the room again. There was a row of people to my right, some sitting in clean suits, others in official-looking robes. They murmured as they glanced at me, most eyes filled with disgust, others with… pity? I didn't have time to analyze it when a secret door opened from behind the throne-chair, and everyone stood. A figure walked out, and I recognized him immediately, not by name or relation, but through his aura of power and dignity. This was their leader, king, or chief.

He wasn't wearing a robe, rather a suit, its black fabric laced with shiny gold lines that shimmered in the sunlight. His hair, mostly white, was slicked back and over, revealing his sharp, angular features, and cold, calculating eyes. He leaned back in his chair, presenting a calm, easygoing manner that was just a facade.

"What's this?" he asked, peering down at me, studying me.

"A *fish*, sir," one of the guards behind me said, using the same insult the gold-banded man had from the dock. "He claims he's from New Atlantis, searching for their trade ships that were lost in the storm a few days ago. His effects are on the table."

I turned my head, my joints like grinding stone. I saw all my stuff on the table, my bag emptied, food and water sprawled next to it, maps spread out and tacked down, my trident resting beside it all. The king turned to me.

"I apologize for the inconvenience. My name is Alan Wynters, named after my grandfather. I'm the Constable of Enoch Harbor, and the President of Cainscion. Your name?"

I struggle to speak, my tongue as thick as sandpaper.

"Where am I?"

"You are in Enoch Harbor, the capital of

Cainscion," he said, smiling. "Now, who are you? I've already introduced myself."

"My name is Dylan Stone," I said. "Son of Chief Poseidon, heir to the throne of New Atlantis. I've come in search of our Traders and their ships. They were heading here when they got caught in a storm, and-"

Wynters holds up his hand.

"I know your predicament, Mr. Stone. I've been there myself."

I shift uneasily, worried about his next words.

"What do you mean?"

He looks at me, his face almost fatherly, except for his eyes.

"You are looking for someone specific, not

just the ships." He keeps looking at me. "Aren't you?"

I tilt my head, looking at him sideways. Images flash before my eyes, of Alex and Abel, and the sight of their ship in a heavy storm, being battered by relentless waves. As their ship capsizes, I force the picture out of my head.

"A friend," I managed. "Do you know where they are?"

His eyes fill with sadness and he shakes his head.

"We usually have Raft Traders and Eastern Merchants every week, but I'm afraid that, since the storm, we haven't seen any ships flying… pardon me, which raft do you come from again?"

"New Atlantis," I say, almost spitting the words. The cuffs dig into my wrists, rubbing them raw.

"I see," he said. "I'm so terribly sorry about your situation, Mr. Stone, and I'm sure the bonds aren't helping. Guards, release him." Hands grab me roughly by the shoulders as a guard carelessly unclips the cuffs, his carelessness hidden behind cool professionalism. I rub my wrists and turn to face Wynters.

"I'll be on my way, then," I said, reaching for my effects. A guard steps in front of me, blocking my view.

"Oh, Mr. Stone, you can't leave yet."

My blood runs cold. My father's words echo in my ears. *The land is death!*

"Why not?"

Something sparks in Wynters' eyes.

"Well, we must help! If you stay, we can lend you resources to find your ships," his eyes glimmer. "And your friend." This spawns murmurs from the bench of people, but a glance at them from me turns them silent. Strange.

"Very well," I said. "Considering I was your prisoner a half hour ago."

Wynters shakes his head.

"I'm terribly sorry about that, Dylan, do you mind if I call you Dylan? Thank you. I've been wanting to change that Justice Mark for a while, but I cannot for the safety of our people. It's terribly inconvenient to innocent outsiders like you."

"Why not?" I asked. Was there an enemy of the land-dwellers, one that will soon be coming after the Raft Cities?

"While most of the Eastern Merchants are harmless, there are a few nations out there that seek nothing but blood and violence. They try to attack us by sneaking in soldiers via false flags or unmarked ships, similar to your own. It gets terribly inconvenient for simple people such as yourself, but you, as the son of a chief, must understand my situation."

I nod my head slowly. Something seems… off about Wynters, but I can't find it. Maybe

I'm just paranoid, my father's words screaming at me. I turn to Wynters and voice my suspicion.

"Are you sure that none of the unmarked vessels were New Atlantean? The flags could have been destroyed by the storm."

Something darkens behind Wynters' eyes, something harsh and deadly, like a warning. Soon, it disappears, and I have to try to convince myself I didn't imagine the threat in his eyes. He sighs and shakes his head.

"I don't know, Dylan. Since they were unmarked, we forced them to turn around before the Border. It was the middle of the storm, so I can't tell you if they ran aground or sank."

My shoulders dropped, but I refused to let the weight settle. Not yet.

"Okay," I said. "I'll stay, but I have to go back."

Wynters straightened.

"Of course, what can I do to help?"

CHAPTER NINE
GHOST SHIPS

Wynters led me around the city in an ancient machine called a car. There were no cars on New Atlantis, just a few wagons and skiffs. I remember the Elders talking about cars, the chief mode of transport on the land. In their time, everyone had a car. The poorest had a small, simple car while the rich owned dozens of them, many of them a type called "sports cars."

I must have been riding in a sports car. It

was low to the ground, painted black. When the guards opened the doors, I saw the glass was two inches thick.

"Bulletproof," Wynters said, as he climbed in beside me. "Everything is reinforced, down to the tires. It has a seven-point-three liter turbocharged diesel engine under the hood, and can push up to fourteen thousand pounds. Nothing could stop us."

I stay silent as we rumble through the city, the people I saw walking around suddenly gone at our sound. If Wynters noticed, he said nothing. I keep my eyes focused on the world outside the window, staring at the huge towers in the distance, with faint, sloping shapes behind them.

"That's the city of Chand," Wynters said. "And behind the skyscrapers are the Rocky Mountains. It's crazy to think how close the water has come."

I drift my attention away from the towers and back toward the wall, or the Border. I noticed a pair of huge buildings, hidden from view when I entered, but in full view now.

"What are those?" I asked, pointing to them.

Wynters glanced at the behemoths.

"Shipbuilding warehouses and scrapyards," he said. "It's where we take unregistered vessels, like your own, and hold them until their owner has been convicted or cleared, like you."

It's unclear to me whether I am the free man

or the convicted one. As we turn, I notice a ship being pulled into the warehouse. I am able to catch a glimpse before it disappears; of tall wooden masts, thick white sails strapped to the posts, and a tattered New Atlantean flag, a trident-stamped medallion over a blue and purple cross, hanging limply from the crow's nest. My eyes widen as I try to hide the notion of my discovery. Again, Wynters is silent if he notices my fear.

"Now, Dylan, how can I assist in your mission?" he says as the car turns, heading into the center of the city, away from the harbor.

"Do you know where else they would have stopped? Are there any other settlements along the coast? To the south?"

Wynters laughs.

"Son, the nation of Cainscion stretches as far north until the land becomes sea, and as far south as the Gulf Passage. We are the only nation on this continent. The rest is untamed wastelands of death and destruction. I doubt your friends would be there." Wynters motions to the driver, a tall, not quite lanky, man. "Shaquille, please take us to the apartments. I'd like to show Dylan his room."

Shaquille nodded, his dark skin and suit a stark contrast to the bright interior of the car. We turned down a road surrounded by small skyscrapers, but still extremely well-kept and extravagant. We stopped in front of the tallest one, recently built.

"This is my personal penthouse," Wynters said. "It's my unofficial White House, if you get what I'm saying."

Shaquille stopped the car and opened my door.

"Welcome, Mr. Stone. Enjoy your stay." He kept his eyes down, averting my gaze. "Your effects have been delivered to your room."

"Thank you," I said. His eyes flashed up to meet mine, but looked back down when Wynters stood.

"Leave us," Wynters said. "Go enjoy yourself."

Shaquille nodded submissively and hurried back to the car and drove off.

"Please," Wynters said. "Follow me."

CHAPTER TEN
SEEDS OF DOUBT

I followed him into the penthouse, and was suffocated by luxury. The floors were stone, a polished, spotty white, with black and grey veins running through it. The walls looked like wood, its dark color making the room seem taller. The ceiling was open all the way up, with an ornate glass skylight not unlike the one in the New Atlantis Capitol. The dying light of day filtered through the panes, falling like golden rain.

Suddenly, a memory washed to the surface. The glass in our house shattering, water rushing in. My hands, extended. The water slamming against an invisible wall, before swallowing my father. A hand on my shoulder brutally pulled me back to reality. Wynters smiled, a fatherly, caring smile.

"I trust you find our accommodations to meet your standards?"

"Yes," I said, as I walked up the central staircase, a dark pillar spiraling toward the ceiling. Wynters finally left me alone, and I collapsed in my room. As promised, my belongings were there, along with the trident, which had been polished and sharpened. I lay on the plush, impossibly soft bed, my backpack lying haphazardly on my stomach. My mind kept replaying the same sequence of images over and over.

"DAD!" I dove forward, arms outstretched. The water burst through the window and flared, like hitting an invisible wall, before another wave collapsed on top of us.

"Cainscion doesn't recognize New Atlantis and the other raft cities as sovereign nations, fish."

...tall wooden masts, thick white sails strapped to the posts, and a tattered New Atlantean flag, a trident-stamped medallion over a blue and purple cross, hanging from the crow's nest.

I wondered what it all meant. Why would

Why would Wynters lie about not seeing the ships? What could he hope to gain? Or did he just not recognize the ships or the flag? No, I had the same flag. But all of these questions led back to the same, simple, unanswered question.

Why?

CRAAASSSHHH!

CHAPTER ELEVEN
SHADOW ASSAULT

The door to my room was kicked open, sending my trident flying. I barely had time to get in position when two people burst through the door, guns drawn. Their outfits were all black, like Wynter's guards, but something was off. Instead of the gold-and-white Cainscion seal, they wore an emblem of an eye peering through flames. We said nothing, studying each other for a minute.

"Who are you?" I asked, slowly creeping

for my trident. Too many times today was I unarmed and unprepared. I would not let that happen again.

"We are the Visionaries," the taller one said through its mask. Also, unlike the Cainscion soldiers, their masks had the telltale flaming eye printed on the temple. The voice seemed familiar, even muffled. It continued. "We know who you are, Mr. Stone, and we need your help."

I was within reach of my trident, but the smaller one anticipated my moves. As I lunged, they jumped up and off the wall. I ducked and kicked my leg out, but they rolled and leapt up incredibly fast. I was now surrounded.

"You're making a mistake," I said. "I know

Wynters. You know this is his house, yes?"

The small one didn't hesitate.

"One of his houses, yes," they said. "But you don't *know* Wynters, do you?"

I said nothing, and the taller one broke the silence.

"We call ourselves the Visionaries, Mr. Stone, because we prefer to look to the future, instead of dwelling on the past. The past is what gave us this broken world, but we cannot change the past, only influence the future. This," they gestured to the room, and to the country beyond, "is not the future we need. We need something new."

Then, they stood straight and removed their mask. Shaquille's sharp eyes stared back at me.

"Mr. Stone," he said, nodding.

I whirled around to see the other remove their mask, a smaller version of Shaquille, his grin borderline cocky.

"Nice to meet you, Dylan," he said. "I'm Tyler."

I kept my trident raised.

"What do you want?" I asked again, my mind racing.

Tyler sighed, "Did you not just hear Shaq's speech? Come on-"

Shaquille raised a hand.

"Tyler, enough." He turned to me. "Dylan, we want to help you find your Traders. Wynters knows where they are, and he lied to you. We want to take him down."

I lowered my trident. If this was fake, something staged by Wynters, then I was most certainly dead.

"Okay," I said. "I'm in."

"Good," Tyler said. "Let's go."

"Go where?" I said.

"You're really that naive?" Tyler sighed again. "Why would we have a meeting here?"

"Because Shaquille works here," I offered, feeling dumb. "It should be safe…" I trailed off.

"I don't work here," Shaquille said.

"Cainscion, like any other company, needs workers. I'm one of them, and so is Tyler." He cast his eyes downward like he did earlier, ashamed.

"Don't you get it?" Tyler asked. "Anyone he doesn't like, anyone *different*, anyone who goes against him is arrested and enslaved."

"So, you're all criminals?" I still couldn't wrap my mind around it, like I couldn't understand the *fish* insult.

"In the eyes of Wynters, yes," Shaquille said. "Now let's go. We've been here too long." He and Tyler pulled their masks back on and grabbed their guns. "Move," Shaquille said. I stepped aside as he fired.

A small, round disk shot forward and stuck to the window. It hummed for a split second, and the glass shattered, albeit quietly.

"Come on," he said, as he stepped through the window, hand gripping the sill tightly. I slung my trident over my back and followed Tyler. Night had fallen, but just barely. Shaquille and Tyler pulled ropes out from a can attached to their barrel. There was a grappling hook tied to the end, which they hooked on the shattered windowsill.

"Follow us," Shaquille said. "Quietly."

CHAPTER TWELVE
THE LIGHTHOUSE

The city was even more breathtaking at night. Dots of light lined every building, perfectly straight in their arrays. The streets themselves were also bathed in light, tall lamps shining down on it, creating a wonderful twisting pattern across the landscape.

"Drop the look, Stone!" Tyler hissed. "Hurry up!"

I snapped out of my trance and jumped down, landing on the ground with a soft *crunch.*

"What now?" I asked, glancing at the sky.

"We have ten hours until dawn. Roughly." I saw Shaquille glance at his wrist and shrug. "We're going to the Lighthouse."

"We can't take him there!" Tyler protested. "Are you insane?"

"We don't have time," Shaquille said. "The plan is in motion, and we can't fall behind. The Keeper wants this done *now*."

Shaquille's car, the one we drove here in, was idling at the curb.

"Get in," he said.

I climbed in with Tyler beside me. Shaquille drove slowly, blending in with the other cars and bikes on the road. The stars disappeared behind the wall, its huge form a towering blade of darkness, unilluminated. Huge searchlights were positioned at the top with a pair of guns on either side, not unlike the cannons on the ships.

"They're sweeping the waters," Shaquille said. "Wynters wasn't lying when he said we're at war. The Eurasian continent got hit the hardest with the floods. Too many people, not enough space. They want to expand over here and establish colonies."

"So, we should let them," I said. New Atlantis only started to get crowded over the last few years, when I grew up. We needed more space too. I don't think it's a problem anymore.

"We can't," Tyler said. The car turned a corner, and we were far away from the city, heading to the mountains.

"Why not?" I asked. "They're people, too."

"No," Shaquille said. "They're bad people. Before everything went to water hell, people blamed this place, the United States, for most of global warming. Some of the leaders tried to stop it, switch to renewable energy, but it never lasted."

"Why? What happened?"

Tyler chuckled, "The Americans were stupid. They switched leaders every four years, in the name of *democracy*." He made quotes in the air. "They weren't focused on the long run; the bigger picture."

"Just the next president," Shaquille finished. He sighed. "We live in the former state of North Carolina. That city," he nodded over to the skyscrapers in the distance. "That's in the next state, called Tennessee, if I'm correct." He turned his eyes back to the road, which had become rough dirt. "Anyway. There is a lot of land here, which the Eurasians can use."

"But you already live here," I said. "They can't kick you out."

Shaquille's eyes pierced me from the mirror.

"Yes, Mr. Stone. Yes, they can."

We rode on in silence.

The Lighthouse actually was a lighthouse, a hodgepodge of metal beams and wooden planks built over a small cabin on the side of a mountain. It was about twenty feet tall, set on the northeast corner of the cabin. The searchlight resting on top of the tower looked unfunctional, the reflector hardened with rust, the moonlight glinting bluntly off its rough surface. Shaquille hid the car in the trees.

"Quickly, quickly," he said, eyes squinting as he gazed along the mountains.

Tyler opened the door to the shack, did a quick sweep with his gun, and disappeared inside. Shaquille followed ahead of me. I took this as an opportunity.

"Drop the gun," I snarled, the tips of my trident barely piercing his back. The armor he wore wouldn't protect him.

"What are you doing?" he asked, voice
even. I pressed the trident further. I saw him
flinch.

"Drop the gun."

He obliged, kicking it toward the door.

"What are you doing?" he repeated. "I
trusted you."

"Why do you want me?" I asked. "You told
me that you wanted to help me find my friends.
But what do you *really* need from me?"

Shaquille sighed, "A leader."

"What?" I pushed again, forcing him to his
knees. "What are you talking about?"

"We're a rebellion, Mr. Stone. We want to
reform Cainscion, which begins with us and
ends with Wynters dead." He raised his head

and gazed forward. "There's been talk. About a legend. The elders among us won't shut up about a story of the Savior of the Sea. He would be born of the darkest hour, his blood infused with magic over the water."

"I'm not magic," I said.

"Funny how you thought I meant you."

I growled and let him up. "It was my father," I said.

Shaquille turned. "What?" The moonlight revealed the surprise on his face.

"He was the Chief," I said. "I'm not the special one, that was him." I lowered my head. "And I'm not even Chief anymore."

Shaquille suddenly lunged and grabbed my arm.

"The title doesn't matter," he hissed. "It's all in here." He tapped my arm, and I remembered when the water splashed up during the storm, right before it swallowed my father. I told him the whole story, the tingling in my body. I looked at my hands again.

"But… I'm not magic," I said.

"No," Shaquille said. "It's something else. And I think I know who can help."

CHAPTER THIRTEEN
THE VISIONARIES

The cabin had nothing inside. It had a rotting wood floor, shattered windows, and a collapsed chimney. There was a door to the right which led to the lighthouse, which Shaquille opened. There, behind the door, was a hole. A metal ladder traveled endlessly down into the darkness, and reached up to the top of the lighthouse. Shaquille glanced at me, and I nodded. He jumped on the ladder and slid down. Lights flickered on as he slid down, and burned out as he passed them. I gripped my trident tightly and followed him down.

Lights flickered across my vision as I descended. I heard movement below, and I slowed to a stop and peered down. The end of the ladder was just ten feet below me, the top unseeable in the darkness. Light leaked out of the doorway, and voices floated on its rays. I landed with a solid *thud*. The conversations ceased. I opened the door.

The stone room was sparsely lit with lanterns, giving everything a ghastly glow. There were carved stone booths in the walls, where some people sat. They had drinks in old, rusty mugs. Tyler was lounging in the corner of one, working with his rifle. About fifty people filled the room, all staring at me. I only saw a few girls, all lounging in the corner, wielding blades. Shaquille, who was talking with a short kid with small eyes, nodded subtly at me.

"My name is Dylan Stone," I said. I took a deep breath as Tyler glanced up. "I am Chief Poseidon, heir to the chiefdom of New Atlantis."

All was silent, until a huge roar thundered throughout the room. They were, *cheering*? The small kid came up to me. His size made him look young, but his eyes and demeanor convinced otherwise.

"What's your count?" he asked.

"What?" I said. "Count?"

"Your count," he repeated. "The number

you've killed. You must have killed lots of Cainscions to get here." I was about to speak when Shaquille stepped in.

"Zero." He glanced at me. "He won Wynters' favor; we had to take him from the penthouse."

"Wynters' favor?" The kid scoffed. What's so special about him?"

"He knows, Collin," Shaquille said, "about the legend. He at least suspects something about him."

"What legend?" I asked. "You mean the Savior from the Sea?" Collin's head snapped toward me.

"That's an old myth," he said. "Cooked up by a kooky business owner."

"What are you talking about?" I asked, my gaze flashing to Shaquille. "What's going on? Why do you need me?"

Collin glanced at Shaquille, who turned away. He sighed.

"Listen," he began. "Cainscion isn't all it's cracked up to be. You've seen the divisions, haven't you?"

I recall the images from Enoch Harbor. Huge warships next to rusted boats like mine. Wynters' fancy car beside old bikes. The shadow-filled alleyways and bright towers.

"What's your point?" I asked.

"We're already in one war," Collin said. "And soon, we'll be in another." He looked up at me, his eyes narrow. "And once the dust

78

clears, it'll be our job to come out on top."
His eyes flashed, and I saw the anticipation and hunger behind them.

"What do you mean?" I felt like I'd asked that question too much. Tyler overheard me.

"Man, with you being so freakin' dense, it's a miracle you float, huh?" He stood up and slung his gun over his back, and I turned around. "Come on, Stone," he said. "What do you not understand?" I said nothing as he continued.

"Wynters, as in the nation of Cainscion, is at war with the Eastern countries, *aka*, the Dadalean Empire. We, as in the Visionaries, don't want to lose our home, *but at the same time*, can't keep living like this. We need to stop being treated like fish scum, and change this government *via our vision*." He paused, letting his words sink in.

"Do I care about the foreign war? No. Should I? Probably, but it's not my job to care. It's my job, and Shaq's job, and Collin's job, and everyone in this room's job, to free these people from Wynters' oppression." He took a step closer and stopped, his face inches from mine. "You haven't seen it yet, *Stone*," he hissed. Rage flashed behind his eyes. "But trust me, it's there."

I took a step back and calmed my voice, silencing the drumbeat of my heart.

"Listen," I said. "I didn't come here to join a revolution. I came here to find my friends."

80

My eyes narrowed as I stared at Tyler. "An uprising is what got me into this mess, anyway." I snarled. I turned to Shaquille. "You said you would help me find my friends. So?"

He nodded. "I will." He corrected himself. "*We* will. Your friends are the key to our revolution, Dylan," he said. "Without their support, we won't be able to do anything. We need men on the outside."

I caught on. "You want to use New Atlantis to help with your war?"

Shaquille nodded. "Yes. I know it, and I think your father knew it, too. Think about it, Dylan. How useful would it be for us to use even one of the raft cities? Able to carry and sustain thousands of soldiers, withstand the strongest of storms, and hide in plain sight? A nation with no borders, unable to be put under a blockade, unable to be sieged, nearly invincible." Then he gestured to me and my trident. "And with someone who can control water, well, you have yourself an army." His eyes darkened as the truth of my father's city reveals itself to me. "And I think Wynters knows it too," he said.

"That's why he took your Traders' ships. That's why he took your friends. They're still alive, because he can't have Cainscions posing as Atlanteans. He needs them, and he needs your ships. He's launching an attack."

CHAPTER FOURTEEN
HONOR AND DISHONOR

We knew Wynters' plan. By using the New Atlantean ships, he could get close to the Eastern Nations and launch an assault, via my friends.

"My friends would never fight a war for Wynters," I said. "Atlanteans aren't fighters, we're neutral."

"Wynters knows what he's doing," Tyler said. "He's not stupid. He'll brainwash em', make them *want* to fight for him."

"And then?" I asked. We were further underneath the Lighthouse. There was a whole series of stone rooms and hallways underneath the mountains. Shaquille, Tyler, Collin, other rebels named Matthew and Ruby, and the Keeper, Matis.

"And then," Matis began. "Once their assault is underway, he'll send his own forces. You saw the battleships, right? It'll be a modern version of the Trojan Horse." I nodded, not having an idea what the Trojan Horse was.

"And from there, he'll just travel the coast, destroying everything the guns can reach," I finished. Matis nodded.

"Yes." He leaned over a map of Cainscion, which was just a seventy-year-old map of the eastern United States with redrawn borders. "So, let's go over what we know. Wynters' major shipyards are here, in Enoch Harbor, and here, in Ash Harbor." He pointed to another city further south on the map labeled *Asheville*. "Most of the yards will be here, near Enoch, although we know of some factories further west of the mountains. But our focus will remain here." He pointed to the stretch of coastline along the Atlantic. "That's where he'll send the Atlantean ships, followed by his own warships." He tapped the map where *Enoch Harbor* was hastily scribbled. "And we need to stop him before those boats get in the water."

"But wait," I said. "Listen." I pointed at the

Great Gulf. "New Atlantis was here when I…
left. Our plan was to travel south and pick up
the Traders near the Baja Delta and use the
Gulf Passage to circle around." I pointed to a
large sandbar labeled MEXICO a couple
hundred miles west, half the size of the
Americas. I traced our route along the map, the
currents spitting us back out in the southern
Atlantic. "With any luck, it's only been, what,
a week?" I studied the map. "Here," I said,
pointing at the faded word FLORIDA. "The
Sunshine Sandbar. That's where New Atlantis
is," I said.

"That's great, Stone," Tyler said. "But how
does that help us? They're nowhere close to us,
and couldn't get there fast enough."

"You're right." I sighed. "I'd have to go back and convince them to change course. Unless…"

"Unless what?" Matis asked. "You *are* Chief Poseidon, right?"

I glanced at Shaquille. He sighed.

"No," I said. "There was a storm. It killed my father." I gripped my trident tighter. "Ezra, one of my father's critics, assumed the title and exiled me. Banished me never to come back unless I found the Traders."

"Why would you let him do that?" Shaquille's asked, his eyes darkening.

"He had half of New Atlantis on his side. He took my father's trident. His title." Shaquille stepped forward.

"You let him take your title. You let him take your people. You let him take your *life*." I gripped my trident defensively.

"No," I said. "I had no choice. My father was the first Chief of New Atlantis, and Ezra said he didn't want a monarchy."

Shaquille took another step forward, almost on top of me. It wasn't a small room, but my back was against the wall. His voice lowered.

"He dishonored you and your name. He's no better than Wynters." I felt anger rising in my throat. I clenched my fists. "You let him disrespect your father. He died for *nothing*."

"NO!" I screamed and swung at Shaquille, hitting him with an uppercut to the jaw. I whirled my trident and slammed the butt into his stomach, knocking him down. Tyler immediately jumped up at me. I swung my trident and caught him in his side, the force throwing him against the wall. Matis did nothing, and neither did the others. Collin's eyes narrowed. I stepped toward Shaquille; my face twisted in anger. I kneeled down as he sat up.

"Listen," I hissed. "Don't you ever say that about my father again. He died for the prosperity of New Atlantis and the prosperity of our people."

His response was a calm, even whisper.

"But are they prospering?"

CHAPTER FIFTEEN
MIND GAMES

I couldn't answer. I didn't know. I hoped so, but were they? No, not under Ezra. I stood up and backed off.

Shaquille stood, helping Tyler up. He brushed some dust off his jacket and straightened up. Matis stepped forward.

"Your response was expected," he said. "You care, but in that moment, when Ezra rose, you weren't prepared. You backed down." My eyes narrowed but I didn't say anything.

"It's not an insult," he said. "It is fact. When the time came, you weren't strong enough. You let Ezra take your country."

I, once again, said nothing. He was right. I didn't do anything to stop my exile.

Suddenly, another rebel burst through the door, panting hard.

"Sir!" he said, breathlessly. "Wynters knows! He knows Dylan escaped!" His eyes were filled with panic, flashing between me, Matis, and the door. "W-what do we do?" he asked.

"That's a problem," Matis said, his brow furrowing. "Does he know where we are? Is he coming for us?" The scout's breath slowed.

"No. He's tearing the city apart, terrorizing

everyone he suspects. But there are patrols headed this way, sweeping the mountains. They'll be here soon."

"If the worst comes, can we fight them off?" Matis sighed.

"Yes," the scout said, after thinking for a moment. "Probably. Hopefully. From a glance, they had standard patrol outfits and armaments, but there were a few more men than standard protocol."

"He knows we're here," Tyler said. "He doesn't want to make it obvious, so he's only sending a few more men. But when the time is right, he'll swoop in and kill us all."

"No," I said. "He doesn't know."

"How can you tell?" Matis eyed me. "The

extra men sound like proof enough for me."

"Listen," I said. "Wynters isn't stupid."

"News flash," Tyler grumbled. I glared at him.

"He's not going to underestimate us," I continued. "He sent out every patrol with extra men."

"But why would he do that?" Matthew, who seemed naturally shy, spoke up. Ruby, who I'm guessing was his sister, clung to his arm. "It makes no sense."

"It makes perfect sense," I explained. "Look at our reaction." I swept my arms around the room. "We panicked. We started planning an escape." I tilted my head in Tyler's direction. "Or an attack. The question is," I turned to

Matthew and Matis. "What Wynters is expecting."

"So, what is he expecting?" Shaquille asked.

"I don't know," I said. "If he wants to flush us out with the extra men, he'll look for one of two things." Shaquille crossed his arms over his chest and leaned against the wall. "One. He'll expect an attack on the over-equipped patrols. Which patrol we attack will help him shrink his search area. However, if we attack, we'll be exposed, and he knows it. So, he'll send reinforcements on the nearby patrols and try to seal off any escape routes. He'll search the area where the attack occurred, trying to find a base, a hideout, something."

I began pacing, my hands making wild motions in the air in front of me.

"Two. He'll look for a quiet escape. In which case he'll probably have…" I stopped, my mind trailing off.

"Listen," Tyler said. "What *isn't* he expecting?"

My head spun, churning like a broiling sea. I was filled with so many details, facts, and information to think clearly.

"I'm wasting my time," I muttered. I glanced at my fists, and the invisible power that might reside in them. I was no closer to figuring that out, much less any closer to finding the ships, finding Alex.

"What'd you say, Dylan?" Collin asked.

"Speak up."

"I said, I'm wasting my time!" I roared, slamming my trident end into the floor, cracking the stone, sending reverberations through the bunker. "You all are clearly Visionaries, 'cause none of you are willing to take action!"

"Whoa," Tyler said, but he wasn't responding to me. Ruby, Matt, and Tyler had brought in some drinks from the other room, and the liquid inside had begun to float upward, as if gravity turned off for them. Tyler took a step back as the blobs floated and flowed.

"So, it is true," Shaquille said. "You have dominion over the water." He took a glance at my trident, which was shaking ever-so-slightly under my grip. "Is it magnetic?" he asked.

"Just the top," I answered, my anger not subsiding. "It messes with the fish, making them easier to catch. Why?" He took a step forward.

"No!" I shouted, yanking the trident out of the ground and shoving in his direction. The floating water flew with incredible speed and slammed into Shaquille's back, knocking him forward. I stepped back and swung the trident in a wide arc. The water soaked out of his jacket and swirled around him, picking him up, back on his feet. His eyes were wide.

"I'm leaving," I said. "I'm not waiting around for anyone anymore. I'm doing this alone."

CHAPTER SIXTEEN
SHARK'S JAWS

The moon was right above my head when I left the Lighthouse. I left Shaquille's car hidden in the brush and made my way down through the forest. I didn't see any sign of the patrols the scout picked up, but that didn't mean I wasn't vigilant. My trident was wet, water beading around the handle and prongs, appearing out of nowhere. My guess was that it was from my power, and it was rubbing off on the trident.

As I walked, my mind drifted. I thought about Ezra, and his power move. Was he in the wrong? No, not necessarily. I tried to put myself in his position. Our leader is dead, and now his son is claiming the title of Chief. As such, he assumes all roles and responsibilities of the title, such as communicating with our lifeblood, the Traders and Junior Traders. Has he? No. In fact, he was unconscious for a whole day, oblivious to his duties. Conclusion, is he fit to be Chief? Certainly not. I think back to Ezra's other point.

"I am not going to allow New Atlantis to become one of the land's monarchies of old. We are a new nation!"

I shudder as the words rise from memory, but I shrug it off and keep going. My mind drifted again, and I remembered Alex, her voice floating on the spray of the sea, up to me, dangling from the Capitol's roof. I can't remember how long I've liked her, but I knew that the feeling was always there. She was the only one who treated me like an actual person, a friend. When I told her to 'dismiss with the pleasantries,' she did. And we've been friends ever since.

I turn my eyes back to the sky, peering through the clearing I was standing in. I can't hear anything, just the soft whistling of the wind flowing through the mountains. It was too quiet. I spun my trident in a quick circle, whipping up dead leaves and spraying a light mist around the clearing. I peered into the dark forest, with the lights of Enoch Harbor glistening in the distance.

Suddenly, lights lit up the forest like day. I'm blinded, but I swing my trident in a wide arc, sending a small burst of water in all directions. It stung like bullets, and I heard voices in the bushes cry out with surprise. Instinctively, I knew it was Wynter's patrol. However, I decided to humor them.

"Who's there?" I asked, slowly moving toward the trees.

"Dylan Stone!"

A soldier appeared out of the woods on the opposite side of the clearing. While his face was hidden behind a mask this time, I recognized his voice and the gold band on his forearm. He was the same officer who arrested me at the dock. I swung my trident toward him.

"Are you okay? We have orders coming from Wynters to bring you back to the Capitol. We need you to come with us."

The moonlight drifted down through the trees. I saw five other soldiers behind the gold-banded man, glancing around the woods, searching. My heart pounded in my chest. Wynters knew more than the Visionaries did, despite their stupid name. He had the resources I needed, and all I had to do was use them. I stole a glance over my shoulder, back where the Lighthouse was invisible against the dark night sky.

"Let's go," I said.

I doubted my decision all the way back. Was it the wrong decision? No, I don't think so. The Visionaries, while they have a plan, won't act on it. I'm tired of waiting. First, it was the waiting back home, for the endless lessons, for the journey to finally cease. Then, I was waiting to die, given to the sea, only to be spit out on land. The land no longer held that otherworldly feeling to me anymore. I shook my head to clear my thoughts.

The patrol brought me around the harbor. We went around to the shipyard where I first saw the New Atlantean ships. The doors to the warehouse were open, lit only by sparse floodlights and moonlight. The ships were gone. My blood boiled. The gold-banded man was driving, and I put my hand on his shoulder.

"Get me to Wynters, *now*."

His eyes flashed, only for a second. "Why?" he asked, his voice harsh.

I brought the trident to his neck, the constant soft *hum* getting louder. "*Drive*," I growled. The car sped up, heading towards the courthouse.

I didn't wait for the door to be unlocked. The wood splintered with a *crack* as I rammed my trident through the dark wood. I yanked it to the side, and the doors flew open with a loud *crunch*. Wynters was sitting in the judge's chair. His head jerked up; eyes wide.

"Wynters!" I yelled.

"Dylan!" he said. "Just who I needed to-"

"Drop the act, *fish*," I snarled. His face twisted into confusion and concern. "I know what you did. You have my friends, and you sent them to *die*." I reached his desk and put my trident in his face, the prongs scraping his neck. "You're using them as soldiers, to fight *your* war. And now," I pushed harder, shoving him against the wall. The tiniest drop of blood ran down his neck. "You're going to tell me where they are. Where you sent them."

He stiffened; his eyes cooled.

"I am not using your Traders as soldiers," he said. "Merely transportation. No one suspects the middleman, ever. By using your ships as cover, I can get my forces deep within Eastern waters without being detected and sunk."

"And forever destroying our relationship with the Eastern nations!" The trident hummed as the moonlight began to dim.

Wynters shrugged. "Simply collateral," he said. "Plus, once we win, New Atlantis won't have to worry about Eastern relations anymore, because it will all be part of Cainscion and our colonies."

"Well… well, what if you lose?" I struggled.

Wynters grinned. "We won't."

I roared and slammed the end of my trident into his side, sending him flying.

"I won't ask again!" I screamed. "Where are they!?"

Wynters wiped blood from his chin. "They left tonight," he said. "About an hour ago. It was a strong wind; I doubt they're close by."

"I don't need them to be," I said.

Then, the gold-banded man ran into the room, along with four other guards. His attitude changed instantly.

"Get him!" he shouted, drawing his gun. I turned around and ran.

BANG!

The huge courtroom seemed to amplify the sound, almost bursting my eardrums. It sounded like lightning had gone off right inside my head. I jumped and crashed through one of the ornate windows. The moon had hidden itself behind the clouds, the only light now radiating from the harbor and the Wall beyond. I had to get there, back to my ship. My heart pounded as my feet hit the road.

BANG!

BANG!

BANG!

The shots and yells followed me. *Get to the water*, I told myself. *Get to the water*. I saw my boat, still docked at the same place I left it. More soldiers came running from the docks, but I didn't stop. I ran along the edge of the dock and spun my trident quickly. A huge stream of water shot up, and I flung it toward the guards ahead of me. It hit them with the force of a tsunami, throwing them back a hundred feet. My feet skidded on the smooth stone floor and I leapt on my boat. It rocked, the metal groaning. I swung my trident again, this time pointing it up at the black sky. Water rushed upwards, yanking my boat off the metal pad and crippling its foundation. I swung my boat around, controlling it using only the water, and headed straight for the gate. It was now or never. I swung my trident over my head, over and over and over, until water began to rush around the ship. Then, with one final swing, I slammed the end into the boat's deck with a loud roar.

An electric *ZAP* pierced the air.

A wave, taller than the penthouse, reared

out of the harbor. With the force of a thousand hurricanes, it slammed into the gate. It stood no chance. The hinges gave way, and the huge doors surrendered to the ocean. I rode the wave out, not noticing the sky becoming even darker with storm clouds. I thought nothing about the consequences of my action.

CHAPTER SEVENTEEN
POSEIDON'S WRATH

The sea broiled, the clouds angry and waves hungry. Just after I passed through the decimated gate, another gargantuan wave towered over my boat. I swung my trident one more time, the hum getting shrill and louder. I heaved the trident at the wave with all my might. As soon as the steel touched the water, the wave broke in half, like it was being cut by an invisible sword. The ship lurched; the lights bounced as I dropped into the crevice created by the two waves. I stuck out my hand and heard a sharp *ring* as my trident flew back to my hand in a whirlpool of water. Then, with one more thrust, I kept my trident pointed straight ahead as the current of my command carried me through the waves.

But where am I going? South, back to New Atlantis, or do I chase the Traders? With the current, I could easily catch the trading ships, but I would have to be careful in the storm. The rain stings my skin as my mind wanders to the other option. If I head back to New Atlantis, I'd have to face Ezra without the Traders. *Ezra has no power to refuse me*, I thought. *Not now, not with this.* I glance at the trident, and the power within me. *But would I be able to take on the Cainscion soldiers alone? With their guns?* If there are enough soldiers to fill three of the trading ships, there is no way I'd make it. I'd have to go back to New Atlantis for support.

But *Alex*. My mind creates a nightmare where she's tied up and trapped below decks as soldiers surround her. Gunfire echoes in the distance, until, all of a sudden, bullets rip through the wooden hull, killing her. I scream, my voice silenced by the storm, as I turn, hopefully, in the right direction. North.

At the time, I didn't know what I had just done in the harbor. I would only learn later, much, *much* later, that I had created the most powerful hurricane the world had ever known.

It was large enough to cover the entire Eastern Ridge, the outer bands grazing the Eastern nations. And it was about to rain hell down on Cainscion; but it was the least of my concerns back then.

I had no idea how far away the Traders were or where they were going. I stole a glance behind me, staring into the blackness of night and storm, debating if I should turn back. *No. I can't hesitate. Leaders stick with their decisions and don't look back.*

The storm worsened the further north I went, like I was going deeper into the belly of the beast; but I didn't sink. I hadn't left the bow, one hand keeping the trident pointed forward as the currents heaved us along, the other tight on the railing. The waves were huge, bigger than any I ever imagined. But with a jerk of my trident, I was able to navigate my way up and around the monsters.

The storm intensified until all I could see were the shadows of waves through thick sheets of rain. I was approaching the eye wall, the worst part of the storm. I could no longer control the ship as well as I used to. The waves were too big, and I struggled to hold us steady. The rain hammered down, drowning out all sound except for its relentless battering. I closed my eyes; I couldn't keep them open any longer.

A huge wave shook the boat, and I was launched backwards. Broken glass cut into my skin as I tumbled through the wheelhouse, the wooden wheel snapping with a loud *CRACK* across my back. I slammed into the wall and blacked out, my world a field of darkness and pain.

I woke to a dark, clear sky, the beginning of dawn. There was no storm here, just the gentle lapping of waves against… against… I took a deep breath and sat up, blood rushing to my head. Everything is out of focus as spots dance across my eyes. Then, I realize I'm in the middle of a nightmare.

"Dylan Stone." Ezra smiles down from above me. "What are you doing here?"

CHAPTER EIGHTEEN
EYE OF THE STORM

The nightmare is real, and there's no
waking up from it. It takes a while to regain my
bearings. We're inside the Capitol dome, at the
council table. Ezra leans back and smiles. He's
wearing the Chief Poseidon robe, with my
father's trident in hand. I will not call it his.

"Dylan, my boy, we find ourselves in the
same situation again, no? It has become you,
disobeying your responsibilities and duties, and
in the end, it affects us all. So," he leans

forward, eyes narrowed. "What should I do, hmm?" I was barely paying attention. He had my other trident leaning against Poseidon's chair. He takes my silence for resistance. "Very well then," he murmured. "Dylan," he said, louder. "Where are the Traders?"

I'm shaken from my stupor. "North," I spat, a slight edge on my voice.

Ezra nods. "Hmm," he said. "Interesting." Then, he slides back Chief Poseidon's chair and stands up. He motions, and a scout hands him a piece of paper. "Do you know what this is?" he asked, waving it around. It was wet, with small splotches of ink around the paper. "Read it," he said. "Aloud."

He tossed the paper across the table to me,

leaving a wet streak along the wooden surface. I unfolded it and began to read. The first word catches in my throat, written in big, bold letters. *HELP*. I paused.

"Keep going," Ezra demanded, like he was the one in power here. I saw the members of the council look on from their seats, and for the first time, I realized that I didn't see any other citizens.

We've just made a huge discovery. The land-dwellers we trade with on the Eastern Ridge are part of a country, called Cainscion. And they are at war. We are headed East, to the place once known as Europe. They're taking us to their enemy, a league of nations

that call themselves the Daedalian Empire.
They're using us, the raft cities, as middlemen.
We are the human shields for their assault.
When Abel found this out, the Man, the Leader
of Cainscion, had him killed. I've sent a similar
note to another raft city, the Islanders. They
know us well, and trust us.

They are coming to help, but they are far
away, coming over the top of North America.
Head northeast and travel through the old
English Channel. We will be there.
Please hurry.

Alex

I take a deep breath to stop my voice from
shaking. Abel is dead. Wynters killed him.

"Wynters…" I hiss under my breath. "Abel was my friend. You will *pay*."

Ezra walks around the table and leans close. His eyes are full of anger and a sick joy. "You failed, Dylan." He stands back up, his voice booming. "Because of your ignorance, our Traders are now captive to the land-dwellers of Cainscion, to be used in war. Whose fault is it Dylan, that they are stuck in this situation?"

Anger floods every vein of my body. "Yours," I growl.

Uncertainty flashes across his face. "What?" he said.

I jumped out of my chair and shoved him back hard. He tripped over a council member and fell with a shout. I stuck out my hand, but instead, Chief Poseidon's trident flew out of Ezra's hand and into mine. I shoved it down into the floor, the wood cracking as I trapped his neck between two prongs, the points drawing blood.

"D-Dylan," he stuttered. "W-W-What do you mean?"

I planted my foot on his chest, ignoring the wails from the council. "You have been sitting here, doing *nothing*, for a week!" Water began to flow up from the cracks in the floor, flowing around my trident as Ezra's eyes widened. "You've turned my father and his title into a *joke!*" I pushed harder, making Ezra wince as the splintering wood and metal prongs cut into his neck. "You don't deserve this," I spat.

"You don't deserve any of this, not even your life!"

I am not proud of the thoughts and urges that ran through my mind in that moment, but I was about to kill Ezra, had it not been for Azul.

"Dylan!" He burst through the Capitol doors. I saw a pair of our policemen, the Raft Guards, closely behind him. "Dylan, don't!" His hands are raised, his eyes full of fear. It was the only time I ever saw him afraid. He sees me, trident raised, ready to skewer Ezra. "Please," he said. "There is another way."

I clenched my jaw and lowered the trident. I take a deep, shuddering breath. "We need to go," I said flatly, my voice hard. "They need us."

"Yes," Azul said, his voice soft and even. "We must hurry." He stands straight and gathers his composure. "But first," he gestures toward Ezra, lying on the ground, trying to stem the bleeding from his neck. "Apologize."

"Why?" I asked, my voice slightly harsher than I meant it to be. Azul raised an eyebrow. "He dishonored my father, he exiled me, he-"

"Needs an apology," Azul continued, his voice never wavering. "And forgiveness."

I turn around, where Ezra is staring at me with curious, albeit suspicious eyes. Swallowing my anger, I hold out my hand.

"I'm sorry," I mutter. "I didn't mean it."

Ezra takes my hand as I help him up. "Yes, you did," he said, surprising me. He sees my look and nods slightly. "But I understand. Before, I was shortsighted. I was doubtful you would be a good leader, and I hoped I would get to fill those shoes." My eyes narrow as he glances sideways at me. "But maybe I was wrong. While every leader has their flaws," he glances at Azul, who returns a nod. "You *are* better than me." With one last glance, he adds, "Chief."

I give him a nod of my own and finally turn to the council, addressing them for the first time since I came back home. Some faces wear looks of shock, others seem content and nod. I sigh heavily.

"Council of New Atlantis," I begin, "I apologize for my behavior against…" I glance back at Ezra, still wearing the ceremonial robe. "The former Chief Poseidon. I ask his forgiveness." He glances up quickly, then back down in what I guess is shame. I slow my breathing and continue.

"As of this moment, our Traders, our lifeblood, are in danger. They are being used by people we once considered friends, if only through trading, in war. Therefore, it is in our best interest to protect our own." Azul senses where this is going, and puts a hand on my shoulder before taking a seat at the council table.

"As of now," I declare, "New Atlantis is at war with the nation of Cainscion for the abduction and inhuman use of our own."

No one objects, everyone understands the situation. "We maintain our current course," I continued. "We *will* reach them in time."

Then, Ezra speaks. "Chief, sir, what about the storm?" I'm surprised at Ezra's sudden humility. My mind flashes to the hurricane.

"What about it?" I ask. "Did you not sense it coming?"

"Well, that's the thing, sir," Ezra said. "It came on top of us." He points upwards, to the rounded wooden figure of the dome, where metal beams arched upward for support. "Just before we saw the storm, we all heard a loud *zap*. Those beams there glowed."

"What?" I asked. "A zap? *Glowed*?"

"Yes sir," he said. "The whole city did. All

the metal beams, rods, plates. Anything metal that was touching metal that was touching the ocean glowed." His finger drew the path where the beams disappeared into the floor, making up the lower structure and frame of the city. "And then," he continued, "Those beams began to hiss," he waved his hands frantically, as if he was trying to recreate the sound. "A gas, looking like clouds, rose from the top of the dome, into the sky. In a few minutes, more clouds had gathered, and the storm began."

It all connected. When I escaped from Cainscion, I must have sent out a signal through the water, probably through my power, the robots in my blood. New Atlantis caught the signal, and the city created a hurricane.

"That's it then," I said, relaying what happened. "I caused the storm." Ezra nodded, dumbstruck.

"Y-yes. The robots in my blood have given me power over the water, which is amplified by the…" I glanced at Chief Poseidon's trident in my hand. "The trident."

"So, you can control it?" Azul asked, his face expressing concern. "The storm?"

"No," I said. "But that's the least of our worries now."

"Wrong," Azul said. "If you experienced the storm over in Cainscion, then that means it must be easily the size of the whole Atlantic. If the Traders aren't in it now, they will be."

"But how will we get to them?" one of the

council members asked. "This storm is dangerous; it tore your boat to splinters!" She motioned toward the docks. "It will tear this city apart! We won't make it past the eye wall! We must find a way to destroy it."

"There's no time," I said. "We have to go now. Ezra," I turned to him. "How much fuel do we have?"

"Not much," he said. "Enough to keep the power on for another two days, maybe three."

"Good," I said. "We're going dark. Put every last drop into the aft engines."

"What are you thinking, sir?"

I adjust my grip on the trident. "I'm thinking we're going on a ride."

CHAPTER NINETEEN
DEVIL'S RUN

My plan was simple – run like hell. We siphoned all the fuel we could and poured it into New Atlantis' engines, down in the Powerhead district. The engines would get some of the speed we need, and I'd get the rest, controlling the currents from Spearhead. Poseidon's trident seemed to amplify my power more than the old one ever did, and I couldn't help but wonder if my father knew it would come to this.

Ezra fired the engines, their diesel roar carrying across the whole city. Azul and Kalama stood by my side as we started moving.

"Hold on," I said.

I grabbed the bow railing and raised my staff. It started shaking as the power ignited. It was almost as if I could *feel* the robots inside of me, conducting the water to my will. I felt New Atlantis jerk as the currents took hold, speeding us along. I grunt as the trident shakes, trying to jump out of my hand. The horizon was gone, just a wall of dark clouds surrounding us. As we picked up speed, the wall just got taller, and taller, and taller, until you had to crane your neck to see the top. Lightning flashed, thunder cracking, giving us just a glimpse of the mercy it would show us. The answer, of course, was none.

I'd sent orders beforehand to not split the city, under any circumstances. Our survival depended on me, and those engines keeping us moving.

We hit the wall, and the whole city was hit by a wave, immediately thrown to the starboard side, pitching wildly. I could barely hear the diesel whine increase, the port propellers most likely raised out of the water. I was half blind; I couldn't see anything. I stomped my foot hard, breaking through the wood and securing my right leg in the frame of the city. Grunting, I grabbed the trident with both hands, swaying wildly. I groaned, slowly turning it to port. I felt the currents shift as the city was righted. Then, out of the corner of my eye, I saw the shadow of another wave, twice as tall as the first. I tried to turn the trident, but it was too late. We shifted to the port, the starboard side rising, floor tilting. I saw Azul and Kalama gripping the railing with their whole life. My head was filled with the sound of wood snapping. I dared to look down, and saw the floor splintering underneath my feet. I tried to pull my foot out of the crack, but it was stuck. The relentless, stinging rain distracted me, and the wood kept cracking, the sharp noise like a knife to the skull.

With all my might, I swung the trident

wildly, throwing New Atlantis upright. But the wood kept breaking, and I felt my legs being pulled apart. I glanced down, and saw a huge crack traveling between my legs, all the way across the city. Realization dawned on me as the harsh rain turned from huge, heavy drops to sharp, stinging bullets. New Atlantis was breaking apart.

"Azul!" I shouted over the shrieking wind. "We need more speed! More speed!"

I could barely see him, only a few feet away. He nodded. "Right away, sir!" he yelled, his hair whipping like crazy. He saw the crack, and stumbled. "Sir!" he shouted.

"I know!" I said. "Now go! We have to get out of here!" He stumbled as he tried to run back to the aft engines. Soon, I lost him in the rain. I grit my teeth and raised the trident. The wind howled, and we picked up speed. My hair slapped me in the face, my vest almost lifting me off my feet. The crack widened, making me stumble.

"Azul!" I yelled, aware that he couldn't hear me. The trident was slipping from my grip, but I could feel us going faster, gaining speed. Azul must have done it. The engines were working again. The city lurched, and I felt us falling off the crest of a wave. We splashed down hard, my whole body shaking, water rushing up between every crack, including the huge fault in the middle. We were almost there, I could tell. The rain was falling faster, the drops lighter. The air was colder, the clouds not as thick. I forced my eyes open amidst the thundering rain, and I saw lights flickering through the sheets of water.

CHAPTER TWENTY
THE ISLANDERS

You see, the thing about the ocean is, it's big. You don't just *run into* people. It must be intentional. You have to actually go *looking* for things. Despite this, we came behind the Islanders near the outer bands of the storm.

The Islanders' city wasn't as big as ours, but it was much more compact. Where they were from, they had to be able to squeeze between all the small islands and land masses of the north. Azul signaled them and pulled us up to their starboard.

"Azul!" I cried. I was drenched in rain and sweat, still stuck in the cracked floorboards. The soft but durable fabric of my pants had torn, my exposed ankle bleeding. "Azul!" I cried, dropping the trident as the rain lightened. I took a deep breath as he came to my side.

"Dylan," he said, glancing at my ankle. "Come. Chief Moana needs to speak to you."

"We're both going to the same place," I growled, as Azul helped me out. "I won't speak until she offers repairs," I grimaced as the wood scraped my raw ankle, splinters forcing their way into new wounds.

"Yes sir," he said.

The majority of the Islanders' economy

focused on fishing and seafood. They had huge nets positioned all around the city, designed, I assumed, not only to catch fish, but also for steering when needed. Two of their largest nets stuck out on the starboard and port sides, which confirmed my suspicions. They didn't have large, wide buildings like New Atlantis, rather, they had a main line of towers running through their city, giving it the shape of an island from afar, with a great mountain in the middle. The Islanders themselves, their skin a few shades lighter than my own, were bent over their nets, busy untangling and unhooking anything caught in them. They didn't carry tridents, like Atlantean fishermen, but they had short, sharp, spears. Azul and I walked between them,

across the narrow gangplank to the city. Chief
Moana came into view in front of us, her robe
adorned with patterns of fish and waves. She
carried a long spear, decorated with small
stones, fish bones, and shark teeth. A pair of
Islander guards flanked her. Azul and I bowed
our heads, a sign of respect. She bowed slightly
in return.

"Mr. Stone," she said. "Where is your
father?"

I felt a pang in my chest. I opened my
mouth to speak, but Azul spoke first.

"I apologize, my Chief," he said. "The
former Chief Poseidon is dead, taken by the
sea. Dylan has taken his place."

She closed her eyes and nodded her head.

"I see," she said solemnly. "Forgive me, Chief Poseidon. I am sorry for your loss."

"Thank you," I said, pushing away the hurt. "But we need to get to business."

"Ah, yes," she said. "Your ships." She saw my ankle, and motioned for me to follow. "Come, let's get you fixed up." She snapped her fingers, and the guards took over for Azul and helped me walk.

"This isn't about the ships," I snapped.

"Oh?" she asked, without turning. "And what is it about?"

I almost said 'Alex', but I stopped myself. I couldn't let myself be seen as just a kid.

"Wynters," I said. "It's about Wynters."

"Winters?" Chief Moana asked. We had

arrived at their capital building, the tallest tower on the raft, taller than our capital building. "The season?" she laughed, and the guards helping me also laughed.

"No," I snapped, shrugging them off and limping up next to her. "The *man*. The leader of Cainscion. This is about *him*."

Moana stopped short, her hand on the door to the capital. She took a deep breath. "Wynters, you said?"

"Yes, Chief," I responded. "He's what this is about. He forced the Traders to go on this suicide mission. He's the one-"

"He's the one you shouldn't be concerned about, Dylan." Moana said, opening the doors to the capital lobby. "You should be concerned about your own."

I bit back my remarks. "With all due respect, Chief," I started. Moana turned; eyebrows raised. "My name is Poseidon."

CHAPTER TWENTY-ONE
CALL FROM THE GODS

"We've made ground, despite the storm. We're only a few dozen miles out from the English Channel, but we have no idea what was going on in there. We could be walking into a trap, or a full-scale war between Cainscion and the Eastern nations, with your Traders caught in the middle."

Chief Moana had gathered me, Azul, and Ezra into her meeting room, along with Islander and Atlantean council members. Our pace had slowed, at her insistence, but we were still moving pretty fast, at my insistence. To keep us together, we'd tied the border sections together and now were moving as one giant ship.

"I understand your concern, Moana," I said. "But those are still our people. I'm not leaving them behind again. I will face whatever dangers come with getting them back."

"But I will not!" she snapped, then stopped. Took a breath. "My apologies, Poseidon. New Atlantis and the Island are close trade partners, and we value each other. Your father understood that."

"My father is dead," I said, breath shaking. "And I'm not my father." I caught a glance from Azul, and I calmed down.

Moana sighed. "I'm sorry. We will help you, Poseidon, but at the point the rescue turns south, or if I feel the casualties will outweigh the reward, you must understand, I will withdraw my men."

"I understand, Moana, and I am grateful for your assistance. Hopefully, we shouldn't have too much trouble." I stood and bowed. Moana followed. "Let's move out. I must convene with my council."

The rain was now a drizzle, the clouds clearing up, revealing the blue mid-morning sky. Chief Moana had supplied some builders and wood to help repair our deck and hull, and had her doctors fix my ankle and help the other

Atlanteans. The waves had calmed too, but were still rough. At this point, I didn't care about what was happening back at Cainscion, whether Wynters was alive or not, if the Visionaries had their 'revolution.' All I was focused on was getting the Traders back. Killing Wynters would wait. I headed back to the New Atlantis Capitol building to brief our guards. Both New Atlantis and the Islanders didn't have an official military, but we had our respective guards, officers, and gunners.

"Men," I said. "We are going in to get our Traders, and going in blind. I'll need some of you on the cannons, just in case." New Atlantis did have some defensive cannons, old pieces of junk that my father salvaged and repaired. My father called them artillery cannons.

"Again, we have no idea what we'll be sailing into, but I'll tell you this." I tried to meet each and every one of their eyes, my citizens-turned-soldiers. "We are not leaving without our Traders and our ships."

All was quiet until someone said, "All hail Poseidon!" His voice echoed across the silent room until someone else joined, and then another, then another, until it was a steady chant.

"All hail Poseidon!"

"All hail Poseidon!"

"All hail *Poseidon*!"

New Atlantis erupted into a huge cheer.

"Start the engines and signal the Island," I

told Azul and Ezra. "We're moving out."

I forgot about the almost-black storm clouds behind us.

CHAPTER TWENTY-TWO
WHITE FLAGS

New Atlantis and the Island broke apart,
with New Atlantis leading the way. We
couldn't see the land yet, but I knew we were
close. I wasn't using the trident to boost us
anymore, but maybe I should have…because
an hour later, everything went south.

I was on the bow when I saw it. Hills, rising
out of the water. A pair of islands. The English
Channel. And right between them, a plume of
black smoke rising from the water. I gripped

the railing tighter and leaned forward, as if it would make it clearer. Something tapped my shoulder, and I spun around, trident in hand. A young Islander messenger raised her shaking hands.

"C-Chief Poseidon, s-sir," she stuttered. "Chief Moana has a message for you." I opened my mouth to reply when she turned and pulled a piece of paper out of her satchel. My eyes glanced back to the smoke. "Our scouts have spotted two plumes of smoke coming from the English Channel. They are coming from two ships, but we are too far out to determine if they are yours. I am worried that, in the case they are yours, we should be wary of an attack. I have ordered we decrease speed, and ask if you will do the same." The girl looks at me, wide-eyed, obviously enthralled.

"No," I said, turning back to the smoke plume. "Tell Moana we won't slow down. Tell her to pick up some slack." With that, I turned and left the messenger staring at the sea.

"Wait! Chief Poseidon!" Startled, I spun back around, and saw the girl running after me. "I-I-Is it true t-that you can control the water?"

I smiled. It felt good to smile, after so long. Suddenly, a memory filled my head, of me and my father. He was showing me his trident, telling me about the ocean. I waved my trident, calling the power. A two-foot bulge appeared on the surface, following my trident. The messenger's eyes widened, following the water. I snapped the trident down, and the bulge disappeared with a splash. Her mouth dropped open. I chuckled and stood. "Head back and give Chief Moana my message."

"Y-Yes sir," she said, running off, her bare feet making hollow *thunks* as she ran.

My heart was racing. The smoke could be coming from our trading ships. One of those ships had Alex on it. I broke into a run. I saw a few guards milling around one of the artillery guns.

"Get that ready to fire!" I roared as I ran past. "We're speeding up!" I stopped when I reached the Capitol building, my boots scraping on the wooden deck. I looked up at the Capitol dome, and started to climb.

My foot ached as I climbed. Up here, the wind blew a lot harder. Our flag flapped wildly in the wind. I grabbed onto the flagpole and leaned forward, squinting at the plume of smoke. I could make out the pair now, but still couldn't see anything else. As I raised my trident, the prongs scraped the meal pole, making it *hum*. My whole body tingled in sync. I felt the city shift, getting caught by my currents. The wind howled, and we picked up speed, pulling further away from the Islanders. I kept the trident straight, aimed for the smoke, aimed for my ships. Aimed for my friend.

Boom.

I froze. It came from up ahead, where the ships were.

Boom. Boom. Boom.

Each blast was accompanied by a flash from the smoking ships. I leaned as far forward as I could, squinting. I could barely make out three masts poking through each of the smoke towers. The white flag on both ships flapped crazily, whipping smoke around. The third ship couldn't be seen.

Boom. Boom.

Fire flashed out from the side of one of the ships, pointing toward one of the islands.

BOOM!

Something on the island returned fire, the explosion thundering across the sea, sending up a huge cascade of water just left of the nearest ship.

"There," I whispered.

"Sir! We see them! Our Traders!" Ezra stood at the Capitol's steps, shouting up at me, squinting into the sun. "And they're-"

"They're under attack, Ezra," I said, cutting him off. "I don't know what it is, but it's big and powerful."

"But sir," Ezra whined.

"What!?" I snarled, snapping my head back, voice harsher than I intended.

"We know what it is, sir," Ezra said, taking a step back. "It's one of those metal ships you mentioned. A battleship, with the huge guns."

My body tensed. "Ezra," I said through gritted teeth. "Get us more speed."

"Y-yes sir," he said, eyes focused on the

columns of thick, black smoke.

Boom.

BOOM!

"Go, now!"

CHAPTER TWENTY-THREE
FIRE

I took a deep breath and gripped the trident with all my might.

"Forward," I whispered. "Forward."

I thrust the trident up in the air, and the electrical *hum* returned. The metal flagpole began to shake, and soon, the vibration traveled through the dome's support beams, making my whole body shake.

"Forward," I said again, and the city lurched, like it was caught on a fishing line. I could see the ships now, sails burning, flailing around like they were alive. I saw the battleship, its huge guns trained right on our ships. *My* ships. The ship closest to us, its hull low in the water, had smoke seeping from cracks in the wood and metal. The other ship was between it and the battleship, protecting it, in a sense. I saw lifeboats from the second ship riding the rough waves back to the first. I tried to find Alex, but I couldn't make out any faces. I still couldn't see the third ship, but I refused to believe it sank.

"Dylan! Sir!" Azul was running across the deck. "We're coming up hard on their starboard side. That will put us-"

"Fire!" I shouted over the howling wind.

"What?" Azul asked.

I knew he heard me. "Fire!" I yelled. "Draw their attention to us! Stay course, I want us between the battleship and our Traders! Go! Go!"

"Yes, sir!" he said, grabbing a messenger, talking frantically, and running off toward the gunners. I felt the city shift, and I moved my trident left, making us almost parallel to the battle. Sweat beaded on my forehead, running down my face and swirling around the trident.

"Fire, Azul!" I shouted as loud as I could. "Fire!"

BOOM!

BOOM! BOOM!

BOOM!

BOOM!

The city shook as the gunners opened fire, waves thrashing from the shockwaves. My eyes traced the smoking, glowing shells across the sky.

BOOM! BOOM! KA-BOOM!

Fire erupted from the battleship. Not every shell hit, but what did, hurt. Smoke and debris were shot up into the sky, a shocking contrast to the blue sky and green island. The battleship rocked, sending huge waves across the bay.

"Again!" I yelled. "Reload! Fire!"

We were almost at the ships now. I could clearly make out the people, my Traders, some scrambling around frantically, some waving and crying, others helping the survivors on board. I saw Cainscion soldiers, too, trying to stay afloat.

"Sir!" Ezra ran up to the Capitol again. "We've cut the engines; we need you to maneuver us in place. Quickly!"

"On it," I said. "And hey, Ezra?"

He turned, looking up at me. "Yes sir?"

"Get the fishing boats. Use them to help the surviving Traders." My blood cooled. "Leave the soldiers to drown."

He nodded, hesitantly. "Yes, sir. But what will you do?"

I adjusted my grip on the trident. "Play god."

Then, I whipped the trident hard to the right, switching the direction of the currents underneath us. My power was amplified from the city's metal frame, and I almost fell off the dome as the city spun on the water.

"Hold on!" I shouted.

The trading ships rocked from our wake, the lifeboats flipping around wildly. I glanced over my shoulder, and saw the Islanders behind us, still a long way away, coming up on the starboard side.

The battleship's huge cannons turned, slowly, to face us. I realized that I never noticed quite how big their guns were, until I was staring down the barrel of one.

"Azul!" I yelled down to where the gunners were. "Fire! Now!"

BOOM! BOOM! BOOM!

The battleship fired first, the bow enveloped in flame. I opened my mouth, but I didn't know what I was going to say, my voice lost over the deafening sound of wood and metal exploding. One of the battleship's shells hit the Capitol dome, completely shattering it. I fell to the deck, the splinters slicing into my exposed skin. I hit hard, knocking the wind out of me. I struggled to stand, but debris from the dome collapsed on top of me. I heard a sharp *crunch* before I blacked out.

My eyes snapped open, pain filling my body. A large wooden beam had fallen on top of everything, trapping me. I grunted and got my arms underneath me. I turned my head, looking up through the crisscrossing metal beams. I groaned as I tried to do a push-up, the debris shifting and creaking. I let out a shout as my arms buckled and the beams fell on top of me again with a *crash*.

Wait.

I shifted my head and saw my trident sticking out of the debris, just a few feet away. My gaze shot toward the battleship where I could barely see it through the smoke and debris. I reached as far as I could, straining under the weight of the beams.

BOOM! BOOM! BOOM!

Our cannons returned fire, shaking the city. The debris shifted, a piece of metal knocking the trident *that* much farther away.

"Ahhhhhh!" I screamed and cursed. I

thrashed around, hoping for something, *anything*, to happen.

With a *snap*, my foot broke through the bowing, weakened deck. Cool water flowed around my boot, and my eyes snapped downward. *Yes.* I closed my eyes and focused my power. Water ran up my leg, wrapping around my chest, flowing across my arm, reaching my fingers. It gathered into a ball in my palm. I reached out again, fingers spread wide. The water touched the trident, flowing all around it. With a *clang*, it was freed, and I grabbed it. It hummed as I stuck it through the deck, water flowing everywhere.

WHOOSH!

Water burst up through the deck, launching

me into the sky. I stood, the geyser pulsing right underneath my feet, like a moving floor. I stood still for a moment, frozen. Then, I spun the trident and whipped it toward the battleship, mid-air. A jet of water shot out from the geyser, carrying the wooden beam. It slammed into the battleship with a splintering *crash*.

I brought the trident behind my head and heaved it forward, sending more beams shooting like spears into the bow of the battleship.

CHAPTER TWENTY-FOUR
CROWDED DECKS

The geyser was easily thirty feet high,
at least. I didn't move, my eyes darting
between the geyser, the city, and the battleship.
It was damaged, with half a dozen metal beams
sticking out from its bow, with one of its
cannons destroyed. I looked around at New
Atlantis, with smoke rising everywhere, fires
burning. People ran around frantically, heading
to the starboard side, where the boats were
unloading survivors from the trading ships.

Something was missing. Whose battleship was this, and where were the rest? I needed answers, and I knew where I could get them.

I lowered the geyser until I could step back inside the ruins of the Capitol. I ran out as another volley from the battleship erupted in the skies.

BOOM! BOOM! BOOM!

Instinctively, I ducked as I ran, a hand over my head. The impacts rocked the city. I almost fell, but shoved my trident in the wooden deck for balance. Our guns thundered in response.

BOOM! BOOM! BOOM!

I ran across New Atlantis to our starboard side, dodging debris and holes along the way. People saw me running, and followed behind me. I was trying to get to the starboard docks, where the survivors were. If Alex was alive, that's where she'd be.

No. Not *if* she's alive. She *is* alive. And she has no idea how much she means to me.

It got more crowded the closer I got to the docks, until I finally reached the border. The trading ships weren't there, just the lifeboats.

"Make way!" I yelled, shoving my way forward. I saw some Junior Traders climb out of a lifeboat, their skin black with smoke. I recognized them as some of Alex's friends.

"Hey!" I said, reaching them. Startled, one of them jumped back, making the boat rock. Her eyes were wide with fear. "Hey, I'm sorry, it's okay," I said. "My name is-"

"Dylan Stone. Chief's son," a voice said. A boy, about my age, helped the girl up and out of the boat. He was wearing one of the Cainscion soldiers' dark blue vests. "What do you want?"

I was put off by his tone. "I'm the Chief now," I said a little too harshly. "My father is dead." Another image flashes before my mind, of my father addressing the council one day. I remember, he had a certain aura about him, his presence…I shoved the memory away before it went any further. "I am Chief Poseidon now," I repeated.

The boy nodded, not out of respect, but something else. "Figured that's why it took so long for someone to find us," he said, helping the other two kids out of the lifeboat. "We had a kid playing follow the leader. Except, oh wait, there's no more leader."

Anger filled my veins. Without thinking, I hit the kid with a hook that sent him to the deck with a grunt. I raised my fist to hit him again, but the girl, the one who fell, jumped between us.

"Wait!" she said. "He's sorry, he didn't mean it. He won't admit it, but it's been scary. Things got rough. He's sorry." Then she turned to him, inspecting the bruise where my fist connected with his jaw.

He stood up and took a deep breath. "Yeah, sorry." The girl elbowed him, and he shifted his feet. "Sorry about your dad. I liked him, he was cool."

"He's dead," I said, forcing my voice to be even. "Where's Alex?"

He seemed surprised about the sudden change in topic, the coldness of my voice, but my eyes told him I was serious.

BOOM! BOOM! BOOM!

Azul and the gunners let loose a fifth volley on the battleship. Our guns could be reloaded faster but didn't cause as much damage. The city shook again, causing one of the JTs to slip. I grabbed his hand and steadied him.

"Where's Alex?" I asked again, after the city stopped shaking.

The kid scoffed, and I tightened my grip on my trident.

"Seems a little bit of you rubbed off on her," he said.

"What do you mean by that?" I demanded.

BOOM. BOOM. BOOM.

My head snapped around toward the sound of the explosions. Cannon fire.

"That's what I mean," he said. "She's got a few other JTs with her, trying to play hero. She got it from you, I assume," he said, motioning to my trident, small streams of water still swirling mystically around it.

"No," I said. "I got it from her."

CHAPTER TWENTY-FIVE
OLD FRIENDS

I ran as fast as I could and leaped off the docks. I stuck my hand out at the water, and another geyser shot upward. I was launched into the air, the water supporting me. I saw one of the trading ships, sails unfurled, engines roaring, heading straight for the battleship. I saw a person standing at the helm, their brown hair waving in the wind.

"Alex!" I screamed. This wasn't heroism, this was suicide. I wouldn't lose her again. I swung the trident up and began to move, the geyser becoming a wave that I could control.

My dirty, too-long hair whipped around my face. The ship was too far ahead, already passing New Atlantis' starboard side. The cannons fired again, almost trivial compared to the battleship's huge guns.

BOOM.

BOOM!

I flinched as one of the flaming shells ripped through the main mast like a hot knife through a net. I saw Alex dive for cover as the shell tore through the ship's wheel and decimated the deck, bursting through the rear of the hull and splashing down violently. The mast snapped, the huge sail unfurling, crashing into the churning sea. The ship rocked back and forth, leaning hard to port.

"Alex!" I yelled, my voice hoarse. I thrust the trident forward, and the water surged, launching me through the air like a spear, straight for the wooden deck up the ship. Flailing, I swung my trident upward, calling on my power. Another column of water shot straight out of the ocean, grazing the side of the trading ship. I slammed into it, my sense of direction lost, and rolled onto the deck, soaking wet. I laid there, dazed, coughing up water, until the ship shook with more cannon fire. A pair of hands reached down and helped me up.

"You're Dylan Stone," a voice said. "What the hell are you doing here?"

"Where's Alex?" I sputtered. "Where is she?" I cleared the water out of my eyes, and saw one of Alex's longtime friends, Kate. She helped me up. Kate was unusually tall, almost six-seven.

"It was her idea," she said. "She convinced the rest of us to help with her plan. Come on, get up, let's go."

"Her plan?" I asked. "What pl-"

My eardrums almost exploded from a new volley of cannon fire, but this was much louder. *BOOM! BOOM! BOOM! BOOM! BOOM! BOOM!*

The Island came into view from the port side of New Atlantis. I never knew that the Islanders had the impressive armament they showed. A dozen fireballs erupted across the battleship's hull, so intense I could feel the heat from the ship's deck.

"Alex!" Kate yelled. "Alex, are you okay?" We started climbing the stairs to the captain's deck when Alex burst through the door to the cabin. Her face was caked in dirt and blood, her hair wild, but she was *alive*. A huge wave of relief washed over me, as my breathing became faster and deeper.

"Kate, what the-" Alex paused, her eyes darting toward me. I must have looked like an angel to her, or a ghost. "D-Dylan?" she said, her voice quivering. Her breath came in short bursts. "Wha-w-what are you doing here?" She ran up the stairs toward me and slammed into me with a hug. I dropped my trident and hugged her back. Everything was going to be okay…

"I could ask you the same question," I said, tears streaming down my cheeks. I held her face in my hands. "I missed you," I said softly. "So much. You were the only thing keeping me going sometimes."

"I missed you too," she said. "So much has happened. The storm scared us, but we still found the trading center, but Abel…" Her breath got shaky again, eyes wet. "That man killed him. He refused to do what he said, so he killed him. I didn't know what to do, I was so scared-"

"Hey, hey, hey," I said, grabbing her

shoulders. "It's okay," I said. "Everything's going to be fine."

BOOM! BOOM!

Alex whipped her head around, where the Islanders were still firing on the battleship. I turned her face back toward me.

"What happened, Dylan?" she asked. She noticed the trident on the deck and the pool of water around it. "Why do you have the Chief's trident? Where's your dad?"

I couldn't keep a straight face anymore, not around her. "He died," I sobbed. "He was killed in the storm the day you left. I was going to take his position," I shuddered, all the emotions I'd kept hidden away rising to the surface. "But Ezra took over. He kicked me out, and told me not to come back until I'd found you guys. Because you never sent a message, and he blamed me for being unconscious for two days, and..." I took a deep breath and hugged her again. "So, I went out, the only thing I had was a trident, some food, and a map. Then, found Cainscion. I-I got arrested, but Wynters freed me. He said he wanted to help, and I believed him, but I was wrong a-and I-"

The ship seemed to explode. I was blinded by the flash, my head filled with a sharp, constant ringing. I felt like I was punched by the fist of God. Then, nothing. Just weightlessness.

When my senses came back, my body was

wracked with pain, and I felt blood pooling around my leg. My head was pounding, every sound and sight was dull. Through my blurred vision, I saw the hole where I crashed through the wall of the captain's cabin. I saw my ankle wound was open again and bleeding. I tried to sit up and noticed my trident had embedded itself deep into the wood, just a few inches from my forehead. I grabbed it and tried to pull myself up. I groaned, dragging my leg behind me. I leaned heavily on the trident, biting my lip to keep from screaming whenever I put weight on my ankle. Then, the boat began to tilt. We were sinking.

I held on to the trident for dear life as the ship listed wildly. I heard the sounds of chaos out on the deck.

"Alex…" I groaned weakly. "Alex, no!"

Everything that wasn't tied down or part of the ship began to slide. I wrapped my arms around the trident as my feet slipped and lost purchase on the floor. Outside the rear cabin window, I saw the sea level much higher than it should be. Water began rushing into the cabin, slamming me back against the wall. I screamed as pain jolted my whole body. I heard the sound of wood groaning against the force of the relentless water. My heart froze with fear as the trident broke free from the wall, sending me falling down into the merciless sea.

CHAPTER TWENTY-SIX
BLOOD IN THE WATER

Cold. Dark. I couldn't see anything, just darkness. It was peaceful. My mind wandered. It wandered to my father. How, ever since his death, I've never mentioned him a lot, never really thought about him, and, when I did, I pushed him away. *Who have I become?* I thought. What *have I become?* My heart slowed as I uselessly pondered these questions.

Cold. A voice said. *Cruel. You are filled with hatred and revenge for Wynters. You have*

become a monster, with a short temper and
deadly outbursts, like a shark.

I felt a searing pain on my back, like I'd
been cut. My eyes shot open, stinging from the
salt water. I screamed, a stream of bubbles
escaping my mouth. I twisted violently, trying
to escape the pain, when suddenly my vision
was covered with red. I kicked hard, forgetting
about my ankle, and screaming from the pain.
But I saw my leg bleeding, turning the water
around me a dark, ominous red. I looked
underneath me, into the depths of the ocean,
and saw the dark figure of the shark that had
scraped me. Sensing me. Tasting me. It
continued to circle, making its rounds only ten
feet away. I tried to stay still, slowly floating to

the surface, trying to ignore the hellfire in my ankle. Then, the shark suddenly swam away, like it was avoiding something.

My head broke the water, giving me just enough time to take a breath. Immediately, my lungs were filled with smoke. I coughed hard, my eyes burning. I looked up and saw the trading ship capsizing on top of me, completely on fire.

"Dylan!"

My head jerked toward the sound. Alex was leaning out the window of the captain's cabin.

"Dylan!" she screamed. "Help!"

"Alex!" I yelled. "Jump!"

SPLASH!

The ship hit the water, the waves rolling

over me, thrashing me around like nothing. I
opened my eyes above the crest and saw the
ship's mast disappear below the waves.

No, the voice said, simply, like a fact.

"No!" I screamed. I dove underwater, palms
open, arms outstretched. I kicked as hard as I
could, blind from the pain. Then, I felt my arms
hit something. I forced my eyes open and saw
the trident resting in my hands. I don't know
what I did next, or why.

The trident hummed, the sound impossibly
loud underwater. I stuck it out toward the
sinking ship. The trident pulsed, sending out a
small shockwave that made my body shake. I
saw the circular blast warp the water, heading
for the ship. Something tugged hard on the

trident, jerking me forward, almost pulling my arms out of my sockets. I pulled back with all my might, but I felt myself sinking, like the ship's weight was dragging me down. I turned as I faced the surface, bringing the trident behind my back. Screaming from the effort, I heaved the trident up and over my head. The connection broke. My body and lungs ached.

I felt water rushing around me, powerful currents flowing toward the surface. I spun around, and had just enough time to register the ship's wooden figurehead of Poseidon before he slammed into me. My body jerked as I was tossed up into the air like a doll. My chest throbbed; I must have broken a rib. I felt myself falling, and I panicked. I twisted violently, trying to see where I would land. I landed hard on the deck of the trading ship with a loud *CRACK!* I moaned and withered quietly, tears coming to my eyes from the unbearable pain in my back and ankle. My eyes stung from the saltwater. I blinked furiously, trying to clear my vision.

"Dylan?" a voice called, muffled. I sat up, my head spinning, and saw a figure with long, wet brown hair stumbling toward me.

"D-Dylan?" Alex said, half kneeling, half collapsing at my side. Her eyes widened when she saw my ankle. "Dylan, w-w-what happened? Oh my god, y-y-you're bleeding."

My breathing became shallow. I didn't take my eyes off the clouded sky.

"I pulled you back up," I whispered. "Ship was sinking. I pulled you back." My eyes fell toward the trident, then darted back to the sky. The smell of gunpowder burned my nose, making me groan. "We need to get out of here," I begged. "Now."

Alex sat up, looking around. "It's gone," she said, breathing a sigh of relief. "They fought it off."

"Fought what?" I asked, struggling to sit up. Alex put a hand on my chest and made me lay back down.

"The battleship. The Islanders have it on the run. It's smoking badly." She looked down at me, her eyes full of relief. "We're okay, Dylan. We're okay." She leaned down and kissed me.

But I didn't feel it. I lost consciousness, and my head hit the deck with a hollow *thunk*.

CHAPTER TWENTY-SEVEN
SON OF THE STORM

"Dylan…Dylan. Dylan! Get up!"

I woke up with a start and found myself buried underneath a pile of rubble. My throat was caked with dust.

"H-h-here…" I managed, hacking and coughing. A strong hand reached in and pulled me out, brushing me off.

"I thought I lost you, son."

I glanced up, startled, and saw my father smiling down at me, his face perfectly framed by the bright blue sky. Azul was beside him, smiling the same, eerily familiar smile.

"W-what?" I asked, my voice uneven. "What happened? What's going on?"

My father sighed, his face becoming an expression of sadness and pity. "The storm, Dylan. Remember? We sent out the Traders last night, before the storm hit. You saved my life, remember? You stopped the wave. Remember?" His eyes widened in hope.

Memories so vivid and feelings so real hit me like a tidal wave. It hurt. "No," I said. "I didn't save you."

Dad laughed, but I saw anger flash through his eyes. "Son, if you didn't save me, would I be standing here right now?" He smiled his knowing smile. I couldn't take it anymore.

"No!" I yelled, backing away, covering my ears, trying to stop the onslaught of memories in my head. "You're not! You died that day, and I never forgot it!" The pain got worse, and it sounded louder. "Who are you!?" I screamed, into… silence.

I was floating now. In the ocean, but I wasn't drowning. I looked around, but didn't see anything. No fish, no currents, no seafloor, and no light.

Wait. There. Above me was the slightest change in hue, from a midnight blue to… lighter midnight blue. The water moved slightly, making my hair stand on end. I twisted around and saw a dark shape moving beneath me. The shark. *It came to finish me off. But this time, I didn't have my trident.*

It turned slowly and started swimming toward me. I fled, swimming toward the surface with all my might. Every time I looked back, it was getting closer. But the light wasn't. I screamed in frustration, releasing a burst of bubbles that rocked the eerie stillness of the water. The next time I looked back, the shark was gone. In its place was a battleship.

My spine cracked as the battleship slammed into me, rushing toward the surface at blurring speeds. We broke the surface with a crash, *and I went flying into the air.*

But I didn't fall.

I was back at Cainscion, but viewing it

above the clouds. I saw the bright light that was Enoch Harbor and another one to the south of it. Ash Harbor, *I remembered. Then, a storm came, almost out of nowhere. It was impossibly big, and it swallowed the whole coast. I couldn't see the end of it. Lightning boomed beneath the clouds, making the very air shake.*

"Look! Look at what you've done!" A voice boomed from behind me. There, shrouded by smoke, was Wynters.

"You," I snarled. "This is all your fault!"

In my hands was my trident, and I lunged at him with it. His body dissipated into smoke, making me stumble and fall. I landed on some invisible floor, like we were standing on glass.

I screamed with anger and jumped up.
"Answer me, you coward!" I screamed, as
Wynters reformed. "Why?"

He smiled and shrugged. "It was all part of
the plan."

Something inside me cracked. "W-What
plan?"

Wynters sighed, exasperated. "Think,
Dylan! Think!" Tyler's voice underlined his
own. His brow furrowed as he looked down
over Cainscion, the storm raging. "I was the
one your father was warning you about, wasn't
I? The mighty businessman who wrecked the
world." He chuckled. "Too bad he never
mentioned he was one of them, too."

"What?" I asked sharply. "What do you

mean?"

Wynters laughed and turned back to me. His eyes were now the color of the storm clouds, the gold lining on his suit seeming to glow.

"So naive. Dylan, where do you think he got all the materials for New Atlantis? Why do you think it's so much bigger and grander than the Island? Or that it has a solid metal frame, not scrapped wood or plastic? Hm? And where do you think he got the materials to build your trading ships, the engines, hell, even your tridents?" Wynters leaned in closely, smiling. "He didn't forge them from wood."

I screamed and swung at him. He laughed and evaporated into smoke again. His thundering, disembodied voice continued.

200

"*And* where," he said, "*Did he get the bots to put into your blood? Infuse into his trident? And* how," *he continued, appearing in front of me,* "*Did he get them into* you?"

He poked me in the chest, knocking me backward with surprising strength. I landed on my back, and pain laced my spine. "*Face it, Dylan,*" *he said, standing over me.* "*Your father is* not *who you thought he was.*"

He stretched out his hand and smiled. I began to fall, down, down, down, into the storm. My mind was filled with the sounds of wind, rain, and lightning, I was tossed around like nothing, my screams drowned out by the wind. I only had one thing on my mind:

Find Wynters.

CHAPTER TWENTY-EIGHT
BROKEN DAMS

I bolted upright. Sweat was pouring down my face. I didn't know where I was, or what I was doing. All I knew was that the storm was still here.

CRACK-BOOM!

Lightning flashed outside, making me jump. My breathing was shallow and ragged. Between the raging sea and thunderous rain, I still heard Wynters calling me.

"Dylan...Dylan!"

"Dylan! Hey, it's okay! I'm here! I'm here."

My mind snapped, and I saw Alex sitting beside me, in an old metal chair. She was gripping my hand tightly; her knuckles were white. "You're okay, Dylan. It's just a storm." I glanced down at my body, which was wrapped in bandages. My chest was bare, my old vest lying on the table next to me. Everything ached.

"No," I said, my eyes still drawn toward the sea. "It's *my* storm." Lightning flared again, illuminating the dark, swirling clouds and humongous waves. I glanced around the room again. "Where are we?" I asked. "What happened?"

Alex sighed. "We're back on New Atlantis,

in my house. The medics fixed you up the best they could, but you were pretty bad. We lost two of the trading ships, but the one you raised still floats, somehow. We got it secured back at the docks." She paused, her eyes dancing around the room, unfocused. I squeezed her hand. She blinked a few times, and continued. "The Islanders scared the battleship off, but then the storm came. They followed it up the Channel to escape the storm."

"They won't," I said. "They can't. It's too big."

Alex looked back up at me. She must have cleaned up. Her hair was clean and straight, the blood and dirt washed off her face.

"What do you mean, 'they can't?'"

"I made the storm, Alex," I snapped, wincing as pain shot up my back. "When I escaped Cainscion. I created the storm to help me escape." I paused. "Well, New Atlantis did. I sent a signal, and it made the storm."

Alex's face was full of confusion. "I don't understand."

"I can control water, Alex," I said. "That's how I raised the ship, that's how I fought the battleship, that's how I caused the storm." I paused again, looking at my trident, which was leaning against the wall next to my bed. "My father did this to me, and I think Wynters knows more than he let on," I continued. "I mean, what I can do isn't a freak accident. It was *planned*, it has a purpose. *I* have a purpose." I walked over, slowly, and picked up my trident. If I listened carefully enough, I could still hear its soft *hum.*

"But, w-what is it?" Alex asked. "Your purpose, I mean."

"I don't know," I replied. Thunder rumbled outside as I remembered my dream, or hallucination, or whatever it was. My brow furrowed. "But Wynters might."

Alex's eyes darkened. "What would Wynters know? Other than how to manipulate and kill?"

"Do you remember his suit? The gold lining? I think he's one of the businessmen from the old world." I hesitated, turning away. "And I think my father was too."

Alex couldn't hide her surprise. "Your father? Dylan, what are you talking about?"

"Think about it, Alex," I said, quoting the ghost Wynters from my dream. "Where do you think he got all the stuff to build New Atlantis? Or what about the solid metal frame, not wood or plastic? And how did he build our trading ships, with the engines and sails? Alex, even the tridents! He didn't forge them out of wood, or plastic."

Alex's face twisted, became angry. "Screw Wynters," she snapped viciously. "We don't need him," she growled. She spun and pointed an accusatory finger at me. "What will he tell you? Huh? Some lies and stories about how he never knew anything!" She yelled and kicked the bed, making me jump. I'd never seen her like this before, and I took a step back.

"Alex, listen," I said. "I'm going back. I'm going to talk to him."

"No, you're not!" she screamed, her voice drowning out the thunder. "Forget about him! Stay here!" Tears began to come to her eyes. "I can't lose you…"

She collapsed against the wall, sobbing, and wrapping her arms around her knees, she began rocking back and forth. "Abel was everything to me," she managed between sobs. "And he killed him. Killed him!" she wailed, her body shaking. I slid down next to her, wrapping my arms around her shoulders.

I was on the edge when Alex whispered,

"I love you, Dylan. I can't lose you because I love you."

My heart shattered, and I fell into uncontrolled sobs, weeping for my father, my mother, who I never knew, and everything else this world had lost.

CHAPTER TWENTY-NINE
GOD OF THE SEA

I remember falling asleep, a shuddering Alex leaning against me, drifting in and out of sleep. Until this point, I never knew I was *this* tired, this worn out. My eyes were red, tears dry on my cheeks.

There was a knock at the door. I slowly turned my head, my throat too parched to speak. Azul quietly leaned in, his eyebrows jumping when he saw the empty bed. Then, his gaze found me, and he relaxed.

"Dylan," he said, his hair soaking wet. "Your storm, it's-"

"I know, Azul," I chuckled, dryly. I motioned to the windows. "I can see it."

"Sir, we must make a move," he said quickly. "The Channel is acting like a funnel, increasing the storm's power. We must get out of here before it tears us apart."

I nod, clearing the fog from my brain. "Yes, you're right." I groan, joints popping, as I stand up. I slowly lower Alex's form down. I take one of the fiber-stuffed pillows from her bed and slide it under her head.

"Here," Azul says, as he picks her up and lays her down on the bed. "Better than the floor, no?" He smiles with a knowing wink, handing me my vest.

"Thank you," I said, giving Alex a kiss on the forehead before closing the door behind me.

The wind howled, impossibly loud, when we came out onto the deck. It *was* the storm from my dream, lightning crackling across the sky, torrents of rain soaking my vest and bare chest in seconds. The sky was impossibly dark, the only contrast being the darker shadows of the waves.

"I've dropped the anchors, sir," Azul yelled over the wind. "To keep us from drifting too much! But we won't last long in this storm!" His long hair whipped around wildly. "What should we do?"

"I might be able to stop it," I said, my voice stolen by the wind. "I created it; I can stop it." My vision was still fuzzy, my joints like rock. But I could do it. I chuckled softly to myself. Well, I could try.

"What?" Azul asked, squinting through the rain.

"Kill the engines!" I yelled. "Let us drift!"

"But sir-" Azul started.

"Do it!" I said. "I need to get to the dome. Or whatever's left of it." I started running, stumbling crazily, trying not to scream from the pain. If I could figure out how to send another signal, like the one that started the storm, I could send one that ordered the storm to stop. Theoretically.

Most of the dome was destroyed by the battleship, but a few of the metal beams still stood, like a dying skeleton hand, grasping for the sky. The ballast tanks underneath the dome must have come loose, because the middle of the foundation was bulged outward, like the owner of the hand was trying to break out of its grave.

"Dad," I said heavily. "You built this. Let this work. Please." I reached the tallest beam still standing, a crooked piece of metal that jutted up into the sky, the end blown off. I gripped my trident tightly and began to climb. The higher up I could get, the better it would work. It should work. I hoped it would work.

Either it will or it won't.

The wind was blowing so hard, I had to be careful to make sure I wasn't thrown off or blown into the beam. I had my arm and my good leg wrapped around the beam. My right ankle was close to the beam, away from the wind. Slowly, arm shaking, I raised the trident to the sky, rain pinging off the metal. I brought forth the power, the *things* in my blood that made me who I am.

The trident began to ring, its usual hum amplified. It was a pulse now, coming from deep within me, radiating out to the trident and the beam. Then the glow appeared. First the trident, a dark blue like the sea, with flashes of bright blue as the rainwater, trapped in its field, began to flow around it. The beam began to glow too, a dark blue-green color. An electric chill traveled down my body, making me shiver even harder in the rain. The water around the trident began to flow faster, becoming almost hypnotic. I remembered when I first called the storm, that night in Cainscion, with Wynters and his guards chasing me. I filled my mind with one thought:

STOP.

Underneath me, light filtered through the cracks in the deck, a soft, dark cyan. A sharp, mechanical *hiss* filled the air. The beam began to vibrate, and I was blasted in the face by a stream of gas. I lost grip on the beam and fell to the warped deck, which had gotten extremely cold. The other beams, the ones still connected to the frame, began to shake and hiss too. Pumping out of their severed heads was a huge cloud of white smoke, hovering just above the deck.

"Of course," I coughed. "The ballast tanks. They're hiding the stuff that can create storms. The smoke." Then, the mist began to surround my trident.

Groaning, I stood, leaning on my trident. The beams were still glowing, pumping out smoke. It must have been regulated somehow, but now that the dome was destroyed, it was releasing everything. I stood in the center of it all, the mist pooling around my feet, rising around the trident. The trident was really glowing now, the water rushing quickly around it. I raised it up into the air, drawing the mist with it. The second it was caught by the wind, it disappeared, whirling away like the storm itself. The hissing continued, sending more streams of the mist into the storm. I continued to hold the trident high, long after the hissing stopped, the glow from the ballast tanks subsided, and the trident's shimmer dimmed.

My breathing was slow and deep, like I was tired. But I wasn't. I was energized, the pain now nothing but a dull throb. I leaned over, breathing heavily, water running down my face and dripping off my long, wet hair. I felt the deck jolt beneath my feet as the now-empty ballasts sunk into the water. It took a while for me to realize that it had stopped raining.

CHAPTER THIRTY
SHATTERED STORMS

I jerked my head up, suddenly aware, as the wind, too, eventually slowed. The sky, still dark, wasn't pitch black as before. I scanned the horizon. Out there, the sky was still dark, covered in the angry midnight clouds. I didn't waste a moment.

"The fight isn't over!" I said to the awed Atlanteans. I made my way over the ruins, toward Spearhead, where our temporary capital was. As I walked, with the trident slowly dripping water, my mind put up a checklist, like the ones my father would use for important meetings.

Find Alex. Check. *Destroy the storm.* Check. *Kill Wynters.*

"In progress," I mumbled angrily, blood pumping. There were lots of people milling around the new capital, tending to the wounded, bartering, looking for family. Mind you, the battle in the Channel only happened a few hours ago. I found Ezra inside, ordering some people around.

"Get the engines back on! Turn us around, we need to head back out into the Atlantic!"

"Ezra," I said. "Where's Azul?"

He glanced up, startled. "He went to get

you," he responded. Then, hesitantly, he added, "What was that? At the Capitol?"

"I stopped the storm," I said, trying to ignore the starstruck gazes from the Atlanteans around me. I felt a tug on my trident. I spun around. "Hey!" I yelled, on edge.

A child, about seven, had reached out and grabbed it. Now his eyes were full of fear, and he was about to cry. I instantly felt bad. "Hey," I said, quieter, kneeling down at his level. I glanced up at the mother, whose face was frozen with fear. I nodded at her, an apology.

"Sorry for yelling at you, kid." I put on a smile. He sniffled and stopped crying. "You want to see this?" I held up the trident for him to see. He shook his head and took a step back.

"It's okay," I told him, my voice soft. "You can touch it." His dark green eyes looked at his mother, who nodded imperceptibly. He reached out with a pudgy hand and ran his fingers along the handle. His eyes lit up in awe as the hovering streams of water changed direction at his touch. I smiled and stood. The mother relaxed; I could see her shoulders hunch as she took the giggling child up in her arms.

"Thank you," she said, her voice a soft, gentle whisper. "For everything."

"Of course," I answered. Suddenly, she grabbed my hand.

"How can we praise you, Chief?"

I was struck, dumbfounded. Praise? *Praise?* Like worship? I tried to respond, but I couldn't.

"I-I don't think-" I began, before Kalama found me.

"Dylan!" She smiled and gave me a hug, Azul running up behind her. "The storm," she stuttered. "It's-It's gone."

"It's dying," I said, hugging her back. "We're safe, for now." I never realized how much of a mother Kalama was to me. And I never thanked her for it. I gave her another hug. "We're safe," I said, mostly to myself.

"What now?" Azul asked, motioning to the people, the wrecked city, the storm. "Where are we going?"

My blood boiled, and my brow furrowed. "I have to go back," I said. My dream came back again, haunting me:

"Face it, Dylan," he said, standing over me. *"Your father is* not *who you thought he was."*

"Go back?" Kalama grabbed my shoulders, holding me in place. The woman had a grip. "Go back where?" Her eyes were confused, full of anxiety.

"You know where," I said, shrugging her off. "I have to go back."

"No, Dylan," Azul stood in front of me. "You *must* stay here. Your people need you."

"This is something I have to do, Azul," I argued. "I think Wynters knows who my father was, before the floods. I think he knows who I am, why I'm like this." I twirl my hands in the air, drawing water from the trident and flipping it around. I sigh and drop my hands, splashing water on the deck. It immediately flows back to the trident. Azul stands, speechless. He bows his head and begins speaking.

"I don't know the whole truth of who your father was, Dylan," he said. "I was born on this raft, like you were." He looks up at me, his eyes sad. "Sixty years is a long time, son." Kalama put a hand on Azul's shoulder, eyes full of sadness.

He continued, "Your father never told me much. But yes, he did own a company before the floods. I don't know much more than that." He finally looks back up at me, eyes big. "I'm sorry I never told you this before. It just wasn't…"

"Important," I finished. "Well," I said,

straightening. "It's important now."

Azul nodded. "If you must go, then go. But please know," he grabbed my arm. "Your father had some secrets, Dylan. Dangerous. Before you were born, New Atlantis had to… build our reputation. I don't know what he did, but he did something. Be careful."

"This won't be my first time," I said a little too harshly. I sighed and gathered myself. "Take care of yourself, and the people, Chief." I patted him on the shoulder and walked out.

"Wait!" Azul followed me out of the Capitol. "What do you mean, Chief?"

I sighed and turned around. "Azul, you've been here longer than I have. Your loyalty to New Atlantis and its Chief can't be matched, even by me. You deserve the title. These people don't need a *god* as their leader. They need a *man*. They need a Chief."

Azul doesn't say anything. The second time in under three minutes I made him speechless. New record. "B-But, I…"

I held up my hand. "Forget about me. Stop worrying. I'll be fine." I smiled, and continued walking.

"Dylan!" he called, running after me.

I spun around and held up my hand again. "Don't call me Dylan anymore, Azul." He slowed, and stopped. "I've wanted to say this for a while, not going to lie." I took a deep breath.

"My name is Poseidon."

CHAPTER THIRTY-ONE
HERE AGAIN

I didn't really know where I was going. I mean, I knew I wanted to go to the docks, find a ship, and make my way towards Cainscion, but somehow, I found myself at my old house. This whole section of Spearhead was destroyed, a casualty of the storm when we lost our Traders. It didn't look any better than when I was last here. There weren't a lot of people, the ones there were milling around the rubble, salvaging what they could, being resourceful. I

loved my father, of course. But he was…
distant. Ruling the city, protecting his secrets,
made him a little like a faraway god. When he
died, I didn't know what to do. What to feel.
So, I chose to feel nothing. I shut myself down,
turning my heart to stone. It's not like he was
always there for me, anyway. The only thing he
expected of me was to replace him.

Or was it?

I left, walking to the docks near the aft of
the city. I walked past the Capitol site; it was
almost flooded. With the ballasts empty and the
deck compromised, the frame was hanging
dangerously low. That needed to be fixed.
When I reached the docks, I saw Alex standing
in my way, a rusty trident in her hand. I

recognized it as mine, the one Ezra gave me when I was sent on my… 'journey.'

"Azul told me; I found it in the Capitol building." She glared at me. "Why are you leaving?"

"We talked about this already," I said. I stopped just in front of her, out of arm's reach. I hesitated, glancing to the side. "And you're not coming with me."

"Like hell," she snapped. She turned on her heel and walked toward the docks. "Wynters killed my brother. He deserves a payday."

"Alex, stop," I said, closing my eyes, my voice hard.

"C'mon, Dylan," she said flippantly.

"Alex, stop!" I shouted. Lightning boomed

in the distance. She stopped and turned around, startled.

"D-Dylan? What's w-wrong?"

I walked toward her and pushed her back towards the Capitol. "You're staying here," I demanded. I spotted my old boat, almost battered to pieces, moored on the docks. I headed toward it.

She grabbed my shoulder and spun me around violently. She pointed the trident at my throat, her face twisted in anger.

"If you think, for *one second*," she hissed, "That I'm not going to avenge my brother and *kill* the man who killed him, you don't know me at all. I'm going." She lowered the trident and leaned in close. "Whether you like it or not." I growled and spun away, not saying a word. She followed me, climbing into the shattered wheelhouse. "I can see they didn't bother to fix it," she said, picking up the two halves of the wheel, dried blood soaked into the wood. She tossed it aside, brushing glass shards off the console.

"We don't need it," I said. "The wheel."

"Oh," she said sarcastically. "And I'm guessing we don't need gas, or even the engine, right? *Totally* useless."

I stood on the bow, glancing behind me. "Yep," I said, swinging my trident in a wide arc, pointing it out to sea. The currents took hold of our boat, and we tore away from the dock, lines snapping. Alex stumbled, crashing into the console. "Hold on," I said, spinning the ship around, pointing the bow southwest. My hand tingled as I grabbed the railing; my vest flapped wildly in the wind. We bucked across the waves, sprinting toward the dying storm on the horizon. As we got closer, the waves got higher. Rougher. More familiar. The rain picked up, the wind howled, and I was right back into the storm. I steeled myself, my ankle protesting at the weight. I wasn't going to be thrown off again.

"Dylan!" Alex called. "We-"

"Stay there!" I yelled back, never taking my eyes off the waves. "It's not safe out here!"

"We won't make it!" she cried. She sounded really scared now. "The waves are too big!

We're going too fast!"

I took a deep breath, wiping the rain from my eyes. I could barely hear her anymore; the storm was so loud. "I made it through this once," I said. "I can do it again." I wasn't about to waste time. Safety meant speed. The first time I made this trip, it took me a few days. The second time, just under a day. If I could make four thousand miles in a day, in a hurricane, then I could do much better in a weaker one.

It wasn't long before the storm attacked. We were maybe a few dozen miles out when lightning flashed not far from my boat, shattering the air with an ear-splitting *crack*. I ducked instinctively, and I heard Alex scream from the wheelhouse. "Alex!" I shouted, "Hold on!"

CrackrakrakraKRAK-BOOM!

Another blast of lightning, closer, just off the starboard side, behind the waves. I jerked my trident to the left, trying to escape.

KRA-BOOM!

A third bolt landed right in front of us. I was almost knocked backward from the shockwave. I yelled when the superheated water landed on my bare skin.

"Alex!" I screamed. "Get down below!" I had no idea if she could hear me. I swiped upward with the trident, the boat lurching over the gargantuan wave. Suddenly, my whole body tingled, the hair on the back of my neck standing up. I immediately turned around, cursed silently, and dove through the shattered glass of the wheelhouse. Lightning.

KABOOM!

Searing heat burned my back as I slammed headfirst into the rear wall of the wooden wheelhouse.

"Dylan!" Alex screamed. She was crouched underneath the console, hair whipping around violently. Through the stars dancing across my vision, I saw her crawl frantically toward me. "Dylan! Are you okay?"

Before I could answer, the boat shook violently, throwing us around like dolls. My stomach did flips as it suddenly lurched forward, and the slick deck became a wall. I fell, tumbling down until I crashed into the console.

"Dylan!" Alex screamed as she fell past me through the shattered windshield.

"Alex!" I yelled. I swung the trident out, and she grabbed onto the roots of the prongs. I screamed as my shoulder was being pulled out of its socket. I flipped over on my stomach, bracing my feet underneath the console. "Alex! Hold on!" I told her. Underneath her was a hole burned in the wood, black cracks radiating outward. Behind her was the merciless sea, waves churning. We were riding down the back of an enormous wave, about to crash into the churning water below.

"Alex," I said, "Look at me." Her frightened

expression, her huge eyes, turned to look up at me. Her mouth was open, breathing rapidly. "Look at me," I repeated. "I need you to climb. Get up here, *now*."

Her eyes widened. "What do-" She glanced over her shoulder, trying to peek behind her. "What is it? Dylan?"

I kept my focus on her, ignoring the hungry, malicious waves underneath her. "Nothing, Alex, nothing. Just… look at me. Look, at me." I readjusted my footing and my grip on the wet trident. My brow furrowed as I struggled to keep hold. "You and I need to switch places. Ready?" She nodded, rain drenching her hair and clothes. "One," I set my feet. "Two, three!" I pulled with all my might. Alex scrambled into the wheelhouse. Without looking back, I leapt through the windshield.

I slammed my trident into the deck to slow my fall, splinters slicing into my skin. I landed on the railing with a *clang*. I slipped, almost losing my balance. The wind lashed out at me, trying to get me to fall. I raised my trident, the *hum* getting louder. It began to glow. I took it in my right hand, spun it down, and swung it back up, hard. An electric *zap* filled my ears, and my body jerked as the boat spun back upright.

CRASH!

A familiar darkness swallowed me.

CHAPTER THIRTY-TWO
CLEAR SKIES

I fought against it. I wouldn't let myself be lost, not when Alex's safety was in my hands. I slammed the trident into the deck, and forced myself to my feet. It was still glowing brightly, warping the rain around it. Through the sheets of rain, I could see the shifting waves around us, while we were still. Our boat was being carried, sailing on a small wave of our own, like a personal waterway.

Behind me, a sharp *crack* split the

monotonous thunder. The deck was breaking, two large cracks running from the burnt hole to the side railings. I kept my focus on what was ahead, tilting my trident forward. The water roared underneath us, churning as we rode through the air, weaving between the tallest waves.

After an hour, we made it out of the storm, finally underneath the blue sky. I collapsed against the railing, exhausted. We were still moving, the trident still glowing. I turned my head, my neck like stone, glancing behind us. The storm was like a wall, where light was swallowed by the darkness. And to think that it was something I created, that almost killed me three times. I shuddered as lightning flashed behind us. I squinted ahead; vision hazy. Ahead, I saw the silhouettes of mountains.

"Alex," I groaned, vying for balance. "Alex!" I stumbled into the wheelhouse and found Alex lying, unconscious, underneath the console.

"Alex," I breathed, kneeling down. "Wake up." I stole another glance outside, the mountains towering over the water. He was out there somewhere, Wynters. "Hey, come on." I shook her shoulders, and her eyes fluttered open.

"Ugh," she moaned. "My head hurts."

"Everything hurts, eventually," I said. I pointed toward the mountains. "We're here." I helped her up, using the old trident as a cane.

The wind was ferocious, whistling through the wheelhouse.

"No, no," Alex mumbled, stumbling. She sat back down on the floor. "Stay here. I'm tired."

"Okay, okay," I said, sliding down next to her. We fell asleep then, to the hum of the trident and the crashing of the waves.

I woke suddenly. The trident's glow was dimming, the waves quieting. "We're here," I whispered, to no one in particular. I stood, joints popping, and gazed up, finding the graveyard of skyscrapers that lead to Cainscion.

"Alex," I said, kicking her foot. "Get up. We're almost there." Her eyes slid open and she stood up, grabbing the old trident.

"Hey, I'm not the only one who was taught how to use one of these," she replied to my glance. "You might have been a chief's son, but I was a Trader."

"Was?" I asked, walking out of the wheelhouse, glancing back at her. She sighed and brushed back her hair.

"No," she said, semi-confidently. "Am. I won't let Abel die for nothing. I *am* a Trader," she said, sounding like she was trying to convince herself more than me. She switched topics. "Are you sure you know where you're going?"

I took the bait, for her sake. "Yes. You just have to follow the trail."

"What trail?" she chuckled. "You're looking for a sign? *Here be Cainscion?*"

I laughed, and pointed. "*That* trail," I said, pointing toward the scorched steel and damaged stone. "Burn marks? Where their battleships cleared the way through the rubble. Water damage?"

Alex cut me off. "Their wake, coming and going." She smiled at me. "Smart."

We continued forward, slowly making our way through the dead city. Chills went up my spine as I passed through familiar ruins, and I could almost *see* the battleships in front of me, my own silent and deadly escorts. Like last time, it took a little over an hour to reach 'shore,' the huge steel wall that separated

245

Enoch Harbor from the ocean. "Whoa," Alex gasped. "What the hell happened here?"

The wall, originally clean and pristine, was utterly decimated. There were huge cracks and tears everywhere, metal beams and plates sticking out at odd angles. The searchlights and cannons spanning the top of the wall were destroyed, only empty shells of what they used to be, if there was anything at all. The gate, what used to be a giant's door, had broken apart and fallen into the sea, laying on top of the sunken skyscrapers, an eerie frame to the city behind the walls. "Dylan," Alex whispered. "What did you do?"

I said nothing as we steered ourselves into the flooded harbor. Everything was quiet; it was a stark contrast to the bustling city I saw when I first arrived. The ghostly silence was deafening. Cracks had formed in the stone of the docks, the metal pads hanging limply off their scaffolding. "The storm," I finally replied, as the boat ground to a halt. We had arrived.

As we climbed out, I noticed that the hull was cracked, near the bow. The lightning strike almost tore us in half. I turned back to the city, Wynters' damaged penthouse in the distance.

"Stay close," I told Alex. "We don't know who's here."

"Wynters is here, and you know it. *Dead or alive*," she growled, hoisting her trident. We began walking through the streets, heading for the once-glorious penthouse, in the middle of the once-glorious city. The bright blue sky mocked the dead city as we trudged through the waterlogged streets; the roads were broken and cracked. The windows of the skyscrapers were shattered, their metal beams bent. Wind blew softly though the streets, whistling through broken windows and trees, leaves rustling. We made it to the courtroom, a hole in one of the windows where I escaped. The wall was riddled with bullet holes.

"Wha-" Alex began, but I grabbed her hand and put a finger to my lips. *No. Stay quiet.* She stopped, her eyes darting around, becoming more alert behind her dark hair.

It was ten minutes of agonizing nothingness until we reached the penthouse. Alex reached to open the door, but I slapped her hand away. "Hey!" she said, but I grabbed her wrist and shook my head.

"*Shut. Up.*" I demanded quietly. I motioned toward the door, which was left open just a crack. "Behind me," I whispered. Slowly, I pried open the door, grateful at its silent compliance.

Even after a hurricane, Wynters' penthouse radiated luxury. The inside was barely touched, save for some broken glass and cracks in the marble. The skylight was destroyed, laying shattered on the floor. Slowly, carefully, we made our way to the stairs, our boots crunching softly on the shards. I found my way to my old room, the one I was given when I arrived. It looked familiar, but there was something I didn't remember. A hole was cut into the window, and a perfect circle of glass was set on the floor…

"Look who it is, Ty."

CHAPTER THIRTY-THREE
LOST VISIONS

I spun around and raised my trident, ready to strike. Tyler and Collin stood in the doorway, guns in hand. I remembered, and I forgot about them.

"Hey," Collin said. "How's it going?" He glanced toward Alex; eyes sharp. He made the connection. "Oh," he smiled. "Is this your friend? The one you so desperately wanted to find, the one you *needed*," his voice turned dark, eyes angry. "So much that you destroyed our entire city!" He lunged, forgetting about his gun. I held my trident up, and he grabbed it, trying to wrestle it away. He was small, but strong. With a grunt, I yanked it away and kicked him in the stomach, sending him tumbling.

Tyler grabbed him and helped him up. "Collin, remember why we're here. *He* said." Collin stood up and brushed himself off, not saying a word. "You're coming with us, Stone," Tyler said. "And you too, Miss Stone."

Alex opened her mouth in protest, but I raised my hand. *Don't*. We made it outside, where two bikes sat out in the road.

"Where's Shaquille?" I asked. Tyler glanced back at me, but he didn't respond.

252

"Tyler, where's Shaquille?"

It was Collin who answered. "He's dead, Stone. Matis too. When you escaped, he wanted to use it as the start of our uprising. But you made the storm. We all saw it." He glared at me, eyes burning. "He died. We haven't found his body." He hopped on one of the bikes and started the engine. "Stone, you're with Tyler." He put on a fake smile. "Miss Stone, you're with me."

Alex grabbed my hand, face fearful. "Just go," I said. "I'm right behind you." I climbed on behind Tyler, and we rode off.

"Where are we going?" I asked over the engine.

"The Lighthouse," Tyler responded. "Only

place that was safe." I didn't say anything else until we reached the mountain and rode through the woods, finally stopping at the ramshackle lighthouse. The only sound was the rustling and crunching of leaves as we descended down into the underground part of the Lighthouse.

The Visionaries.

Like last time, silence descended over the room like a wave when I entered. I stood my trident up next to me, the sound of metal on steel making a powerful *clang*. Alex stood behind me, eyes darting everywhere.

"Hear ye!" Collin cried, voice full of sarcasm. "It's Dylan Stone, ruler of the oceans. He's back! The Savior of the Sea!" The announcement didn't warrant an applause. It wasn't supposed to.

"He wasn't lying," Tyler added. "Bring him out."

I knew who *he* was, even before two Visionaries disappeared down a hallway and came back a few minutes later with a hooded body. They set him up in a chair, in the middle of the room. Tyler yanked the hood off his head, revealing Wynters' stark white hair.

"Ah! Dylan!" Wynters smiles. If he saw Alex out of the corner of his eye, he never looked at her. "I knew you would come back. I told them!" He laughed and winked. "And I know why you came back, too. It was just a matter of time." He chuckled again.

Alex stepped forward, and shoved the trident in his face. "Stop doing that," she growled. He looked surprised, as if seeing her for the first time. Despite being the only one in the room tied to a chair, Wynters was the only one in the room with control. And he knew it.

"My father," I said, drawing his attention back to me. "You knew him. That's why you didn't kill me. You know what I am."

Wynters looked up at me, the low light giving his face a dark yellow glow. "I knew your father. I owned the company he worked at. Those *things* in your blood? They're called nanobots. And water? Water is a polar molecule."

"Get to the point," I growled.

Wynters glanced at me, jaw clenched. "Water consists of two hydrogen atoms and one oxygen atom. That is what gives it its polarity. That means that it has small magnetic properties, like a microscopic magnet. Your blood," he nodded toward my arm. "Along with the nanobots, takes advantage of water's polarity in order to *manipulate* it."

He nodded again, toward the trident. "The trident was solely your father's. He put the same nanobots into the core. Being metal, the trident is an amplifier." He chuckled.

"But," Wynters tsked. "It wasn't for him. It was for you. The whole *Savior of the Sea*?" He laughed. The Visionaries stayed silent. "A tale. When the floods came, it was the perfect time, albeit with a price." He leaned up, as far as he could.

"There is a plan, Dylan. It's bigger than you. You just have to," his eyes widened, "Open your eyes. Ha! Open your eyes, Dylan!" He rattled around in his chair, making me jump. "There is a whole future built around you. You have no idea how valuable you are, Dylan. You are... you are... you-"

I cut him off. "My name is Poseidon."

He smiled. "Yes, yes, it is. And with that, Operation Olympians is underway."

I raised the trident, making it *hum* and glow softly.

"What's Operation Olympians?" I demanded, my voice hard. "Tell me."

Wynters' face turned sheepish, like he was a child. "Ooh, I can't tell you that. You'll have to figure that out for yourself. But what I *can* tell you, is that you're not the only one," he said, winking. Then, he leaned toward Collin. "I believe our deal is satisfied," he said.

"Wait, what deal?" Alex snapped. "There wasn't a deal."

"Not between us," Collin snapped back, stepping forward. "In exchange for his freedom, Wynters promised us *him*." A few Visionaries came around and stood behind us, blocking the door to the ladder.

"Thank you, Collin," Wynters said.

"Shut up," he snapped. "We're not done with you."

Wynters' smile faltered. "Excuse me?"

"I said, shut up!" Collin roared, punching Wynters. His head snapped to the side. "You're next, whitehead." Collin's eyes darted back to me. "Get 'em," he said. I heard the *ring* of blades being drawn, and the *click* of a cocking gun.

There wasn't a lot of water down here. We had to escape. "Alex," I whispered, gripping my trident. "*Run.*"

I immediately slammed my trident down into the stone floor, sending an ear-splitting *clang* reverberating throughout the small room. The Visionaries were stunned, and I grabbed Alex and shoved my way through, almost throwing her up the ladder.

"Go!" I shouted. I looked back and, through the chaos, saw Wynters stand, his bonds disintegrating into shadows. He fixed his impeccably clean suit, catching my eye. He smiled, before disappearing down the dark hallway. Collin stood, eyes full of anger, gun raised.

BANG! I ducked, and the bullet slammed into the stone beside me. I scrambled up the ladder, the other Visionaries following me.

"Dylan!" Alex leaned down into the hole and stuck out her hand. I grabbed it and hefted myself up.

"Run!" I said, hearing the Visionaries roar and curse behind me. We ran through the woods, branches snapping underneath our feet.

My mind kept replaying flashbacks of the first time I did this, the only light coming from the moon, being caught by Wynters' scouts, infuriated by the Visionaries inability to act.

"Dylan," Alex panted. "Where are we going?" I could tell she was angry. She wanted Wynters dead.

"Out," I responded, not slowing down. "I'm done with this place."

She cut in front of me and shoved me hard, throwing me to the ground. "Well, I'm not," she cried, tears coming to her eyes. "Wynters is still alive. You're saying we came all this way, through a *freaking hurricane*, which almost killed us, by the way, just to get shot at by some lunatics and let him escape?" She growled in frustration as I climbed to my feet.

"Alex, we don't have time for this," I said sternly. "Let's go."

"Where, Dylan?!" she cried. "Where? Where else in this godforsaken world can we go? Tell me!" She was shaking, tears were streaming down her face. Behind her, I heard shouts and saw dark shapes moving through the forest. We couldn't hide here in the middle of the day.

I took a quick, deep breath. "East," I said. "Wynters' enemy is our friend. Now let's go. Now."

She heard the voices behind her and ran.

"Our boat won't make it through another trip," she said. "Where are we going to find another one?"

"Wynters only sent out two trading ships," I
answered.

CHAPTER THIRTY-FOUR
THE EARTH SHAKER

I didn't know where we were going, to be
honest. I didn't get all the information from
Wynters either. The answers he gave me
weren't answers, just predecessors to more
questions. What was Operation Olympians?
What did he mean *I wasn't the only one*? Why
did my father work for him? Why was I even-

BANG!

A gunshot blew a tree apart just inches from
my head, splinters slicing into my cheeks. I

shook my head and cleared my vision. "Head down to the docks," I told Alex. "There should be a warehouse, near the wall. It should be intact, and there's a ship in there. Go!" I said, slowing down.

"Wait!" Alex skidded to a halt. "Where are *you* going?"

"To draw them off," I answered breathlessly. "Now go." She took off, glancing back only once. I turned to face the moving silhouettes, anger rising. "Showtime."

I slammed the trident into the ground, releasing another shockwave. I focused it this time, sending the tremor straight up the mountain toward the Visionaries. The Visionaries cried out as the whole forest shook, the sound of falling rocks turning to thunder. I turned around and kept running, flying through the trees. Gunshots, each one the cry of a broken promise, chased me. My bad ankle throbbed when I ran, but I had to ignore it. We weren't far from the city, but there was no way I could outrun them, especially if they were on the bikes. When the panic cleared, an idea surfaced. If I could send shockwaves through the ground, then couldn't I…?

I slammed the trident into the ground again, releasing another shockwave. But this time, I launched myself in the air, like I was shot from a cannon. My arms flailed wildly. I saw Alex off to my left, breaking through the tree line and sprinting through the streets. She'd make it to the warehouse in maybe five minutes. She needed more time. I twisted around in midair, and heaved the trident back at the Visionaries. It landed right in front of them with a *boom*, and the nearest ones were thrown back. The others started firing as I began to fall.

I stuck out my hands and closed my eyes. My body shook and released a shockwave right before I hit the road. Dust, leaves, and rubble flew up around me as I rolled and jumped to my feet. I had gained lots of ground, and if I kept them on me, Alex would find the ship. I raised my hand, and a few seconds later, the trident flew back to my palm with a metallic *ring*. The Visionaries shouted, gunfire echoing across the mountainside.

"Come on!" I yelled, as loudly as I could. "Is that all you've got?"

"'Maybe, but it's not all I got."

I was yanked backwards, like my body was tied to some invisible string. I was forced to my knees, skin scraping along the road, until I reached the feet of Wynters.

"You," I snarled. "I'm going to kill you."

He laughed. "Oh, I doubt that." He brought his hand up, and the force lifted me up, until my boots were barely touching the ground. "It's not your job to."

"Like hell it isn't," I growled. I tried to struggle, but I couldn't move. Wynters still had his hand, palm up, fingers curled.

"My boy," he said. "There are still lots of

things you don't know. You don't even know the mythology behind your own name, do you?" I said nothing. Wynters tsked.

"A long, *long* time before the floods, there was a place, a civilization, called Ancient Greece." He began walking in circles around me, like a shark, as I dangled helplessly. "They worshipped the gods of Olympus. Their deities numbered in the dozens, if not hundreds. There was a god for every aspect of life and nature." He paused, coming back around again. "Most notably were the big three. The three most powerful gods. No one rivaled them." He continued walking again, each word punctuated by the sharp *clack* of his boots on stone.

"Zeus."

Clack.

"Hades."

Clack.

"And you, Poseidon."

Clack! He stopped to face me.

"You aren't a one-off," he said. "A mistake. You, my friend, *you* have a purpose. A *mission*," he clenched his fist, and the force around my body tightened, making me cry out in pain. "*That's* what Operation Olympians is."

He leaned in close, his eyes impossibly dark out in the daylight. "Your destiny. Yours, and your brother's." He smiled, as shadows gathered around him as he descended into an alleyway. He straightened.

"Another word of advice, my friend." He

271

grinned as the shadows swallowed him. "If you want to find a god, you must first find his kingdom."

BANG!

Bullets sparked on the road around me, as Wynters vanished into the shadows. At first, I was frozen with fear.

"Get him!"

BANG! BANG!

Sparks flashed as I broke into a sprint, heading for the docks. *Alex, be there*, I prayed. *Be there.* I could spot the warehouse now, just off in the distance. It was close enough to the wall that it was spared from my storm's worst. Then, I saw the front doors open, and a boat rolled out. No, not a boat. A *ship*. I smiled when I saw Alex standing in the crow's nest of the third trading ship, the New Atlantis flag unraveling in the wind. I turned sharply, making a beeline for the docks.

"There he is!" voices shouted from behind me, gunshots echoing and bouncing through the dead city. I stuck out my trident and yanked it back towards me. A beam of water shot out of the harbor, some three hundred feet away. I spun out of the way and let it splash down behind me, giving a few seconds of cover from the Visionaries.

"Dylan, stop!" Tyler's voice cut through the air. I don't know why, but my feet stopped moving. I tightened my lips and clenched my fists.

"What?" I replied, keeping my back to him.

"Why did you do this?" he asked. "You promised us you would help, then you left us, and sent a storm to kill us. Why?"

"I'm sorry about the storm," I said, glancing over my shoulder. "It wasn't meant for you."

"But we still got hit," I heard him say. "So, answer me. Why?"

I didn't say anything. Behind me, I heard someone cock a gun. I shook my head. "Goodbye." I slammed my trident into the ground, cracking the road and launching me into the air. I whipped the trident upwards, and a geyser of water carried me to the trading ship.

I landed on the deck as we sailed through the gates of Cainscion for the last time.

"You said east," Alex said, sliding down the ship's rigging. "Where east, exactly? Back home?" I saw a sparkle of hope in her eyes. I ignored it.

"No," I said. "Wynters said I wasn't the only one. There are two more: Zeus and Hades."

"Who are they?" she asked, climbing up to the wheel.

"I don't know," I said. "But… but I think they're like me," I mumbled, looking down at my hands.

"What does that mean?" she said, weaving the ship through the graveyard maze.

"It means I have to go," I said, standing behind her. "I don't have another choice."

"Yes, you do," she said, turning around. "Go home. Forget about this. Why do you even trust Wynters anyway? He's nothing but a liar."

"He never lied," I said. "And you know it." I turned away, looking back at the ravaged wall. "I can't ignore this. He said I was… created for a reason. I have these powers for a reason. I can't let that go."

"Maybe you should," Alex said, spinning me back around and grabbing my wrists. "We need to go back anyway. You're still Chief."

I smiled sadly and shrugged. "No, I'm not," I said, tilting my head down. "Azul is. He knows I'm not coming back for a while."

Alex sighed, fresh out of arguments. "Fine,"

she said, pulling away. "But wherever you go, I'm with you."

I opened my mouth to protest. "Fine," I said, surprised at my own words. "You can come."

She smiled and took my hand. "So," she whispered in my ear. "If you're not Chief anymore, what does that make you? Just regular old Dylan?" I felt her smile on my cheek as her hand ran up my chest.

"No," I said, taking a deep breath, breathing in the air from the ocean. My home.

"I am Poseidon."

EPILOGUE

"Poseidon has awakened. And with him, Atlantis," the man said. "Do you know what this means?" He usually stands in a way that demands authority, obedience. But not here, not in this room. Not the room with the obsidian throne.

Hades laughed, a dry, sour crackle that sends chills down the man's spine.

"It means my father is *dead*," he hissed. He jerked his head up, revealing the pasty white skin and deep red eyes hidden underneath pitch black hair. Hades laughed again, harder. "And it has begun. Finally, *finally*." He opened his hands, palms facing down. The ground began to shake, an electronic *whine* filling the air. "We will get to do what we were created to do."

With one last, thunderous *boom*, a grinning Hades leaned back in his chair, dust and soot raining from the ceiling of the cavern.

"Send word to the Daedalians. They must already know the Earth Shaker is back, if everything has gone according to the plan." He rubs his chin, then snaps his fingers, creating a short flash of sparks illuminating the ghastly cave for a second. "If we are to win this war, we must not fight. How is the puppet?"

"Cainscion, sir? Destroyed. Poseidon took it out with a storm." The man would not show fear, but his voice cracked, ever so slightly. "Their war with the Daedalians has ground to a halt."

"Yes," Hades mumbled. "Good. And Wynters?"

"Unknown, sir," the man said. "Poseidon went back to Cainscion, most likely for revenge or information. We believed he escaped."

"Hmmm," Hades mumbled. "Contain him," he said. "Until the time is right. He is an important piece in this game, with a special role. He is our step to what's coming next. The plan is falling perfectly."

"What's next, sir?" The man asked, trying not to sound timid.

Hades fell silent and leaned forward in his throne. "What's next?" he repeated, softly. "What's next? Well, I'll tell you what's next!" Hades roared, shaking the cavern, making rocks tumble. When it stopped, Hades' laugh could be heard over the falling rocks. "Next, comes the apokálypsis."

"The... what?" The man stuttered. "Didn't the world already experience the apocalypse?" Hades grinned.

"I'm not talking about the end of the world, but the creation of a new one." The cavern began to shake again, making the man cry out. Hades cackled with laughter.

"*My* world!"

ACKNOWLEDGEMENTS

The road to publishing has been long and difficult, with lots of potholes along the way. However, I must thank a few people who helped set me on this path and those who made it easier.

First, I'd like to thank my family, especially my brother. We started babbling about the books Mom read to us when we were toddlers. Ever since then, you've been my mirror, the one exactly the same, and yet completely different.

Mom, you encouraged us to talk about our own ideas back then, even if it was just to make us fall asleep. And Dad, you are always there for me, as a father and a coach. I appreciate everything you've done for me and with me. I couldn't ask for more.

I couldn't and wouldn't be here today if not for my third and fourth grade teacher, Mr. Brucell. You were the one who really dove deep into literacy and helped me find the joy of a story. I still remember the books we read together as a class and all the fun we had doing it. You were the one who first saw my potential and pointed me down this crazy, unpredictable, awesome path.

I'd also like to thank my seventh-grade teacher, Ms. Green. I started writing by then, working on the 'great American novel' with my best friend and brother. Ms. Green, I thank you for the time you spent reading the first few drafts of it and the effort you put into giving feedback and encouragement.